MONKEY HUNTING

CRISTINA GARCÍA

MONKEY HUNTING

ALFRED A. KNOPF  NEW YORK 2003

Library of Congress Cataloging-in-Publication Data
García, Cristina, [date]
Monkey hunting / Cristina García. — 1st ed.
p.   cm.
ISBN 0-375-41056-2 (alk. paper)
1. Chinese—Cuba—Fiction.   2. Cuban Americans—Fiction.
3. Slavery—Fiction.   4. China—Fiction.   5. Cuba—Fiction.
I. Title.

PS3557.A66 M66 2003
813'.54—dc21   2002035916

Manufactured in the United States of America
First Edition

For José Garriga

I, Old Monkey, can with this pair
of fiery eyes and diamond pupils,
discern good and evil.

—**WU CH'ÊNG-ÊN**
The Journey to the West

CONTENTS

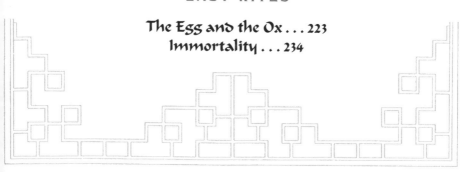

FAMILY TREE

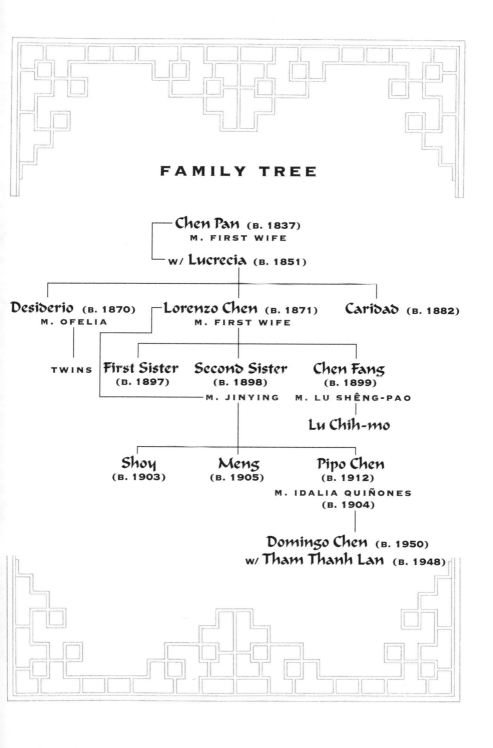

Chen Pan (B. 1837)
M. FIRST WIFE

w/ Lucrecia (B. 1851)

Desiderio (B. 1870)   Lorenzo Chen (B. 1871)   Caridad (B. 1882)
M. OFELIA   M. FIRST WIFE

TWINS   First Sister   Second Sister   Chen Fang
             (B. 1897)   (B. 1898)   (B. 1899)
                          M. JINYING   M. LU SHÊNG-PAO

Lu Chih-mo

Shoy   Meng   Pipo Chen
(B. 1903)   (B. 1905)   (B. 1912)
                                    M. IDALIA QUIÑONES
                                    (B. 1904)

Domingo Chen (B. 1950)
w/ Tham Thanh Lan (B. 1948)

ORIGINS

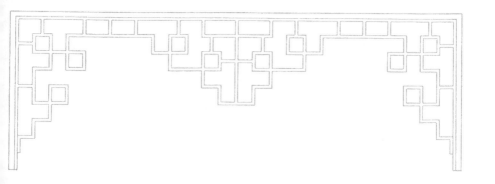

Prologue

AMOY, CHINA
(1857)

emptations were plentiful in Amoy. At the circus, Chen Pan watched as the trapeze artist swung from one end of her sagging tent to another in a crimson streak. He followed her soarings, the arc of her willow eyebrows, her delicate steps along the fragile-seeming tightrope. She wore a spangled bodice and knee-high leather boots. Her legs were straight as bamboo. She was beautiful, this Fire Swan, calm and disdainful, taller than any woman Chen Pan had ever seen.

Only a week ago he'd left his village by the J—— River to look for work in the city. Winter rains had flooded his wheat fields, rotting the stalks already choked with darnel. Bandits were roaming the countryside, setting fires and stealing horses. How far away all this seemed to him now.

Outside the circus tent, the hills of Amoy scalloped down to the rim of the sea. Foreign sailors patrolled the port in their tasseled uniforms. Bedraggled men hauled crates and burlap bundles, loading the British ships. Near the docks, a tavern painted with scenes of spring served warmed wine from jade jars. The owner coaxed Chen Pan to a back room lined with silk cushions. The night before, he'd gotten lucky throwing dice against a barge captain. The winnings were still in his pocket.

A musician was playing an old-fashioned ch'in, *singing the lament of a forgotten mistress. Dancing girls in scarlet skirts beckoned to him like a sea of peonies. Dishes of peas with aniseed appeared at his table with a generous dipping of wine. The owner offered Chen Pan a carved opium pipe. He took one puff, then another. Soon the sweet hot smoke had him searching the clouds for immortals. In the delicate haze of the ensuing hours, his gambling gold slowly vanished in the arms of a lush dancing girl.*

The following afternoon, a slope-shouldered man with drooping whiskers invited Chen Pan for tea. What more did he have to lose? The tea was hot and heavily sugared. There were sweetmeats and bean paste cakes. The man wore a Western-style suit and a ring on his little finger, flecked with diamond chips. His age was impossible to guess. Chen Pan wanted to believe everything he said. How the drinking water in Cuba was so rich with minerals that a man had twice his ordinary strength (and could stay erect for days). That the Cuban women were eager and plentiful, much lovelier than the Emperor's concubines. That even the river fish jumped, unbidden, into frying pans. Suddenly the world seemed larger and more unfathomable than Chen Pan had imagined.

"Spit the country dirt from your mouth!" the man in the Western suit pressed him. "You need to act while you're young! What? Are you waiting for peaches to fall from heaven?" He counted out eight Mexican coins as a deposit, pledged four pesos more a month for eight years. "And remember," he said, with a quick roll of his shoulders, "one foreign year elapses twice as fast as a Chinese one!"

But what if the opposite were true, Chen Pan worried. His father had told him once that a Chinese mile was only one-third as long as an English one. If this held true for time as well, he would be gone for twenty-four years.

Chen Pan tried to picture Cuba, an island—the man in the Western suit explained—that was many times the size of Amoy. If all went well, Chen Pan speculated, he could return home a wealthy man, perhaps a stronger man if the story about the drinking water wasn't a lie. Then he'd build a splendid house by the river, huge and on stilts, better than any in his village's memory. He'd buy two or three *more wives, comely and fecund as hens, found his own dynasty. At the end of his life there would be four generations of Chens living under one roof.*

There would be tales to tell, too, enough to fill many evenings with his adventures. If only his poor father could be alive to hear them!

It was winter and fiercely cold. The sun had declined its duty by midafternoon. In Cuba, Chen Pan was assured, the air was as tepid as a summer bath all year long. No more snow or bitter winds. Chen Pan didn't suffer his decision. This time, he believed, the odds were in his favor. He signed the contract, unrolled with a flourish on the little tabletop. Then Chen Pan took his first coin, still warm from the hands of the man in the Western suit. He would go beyond the edge of the world to Cuba.

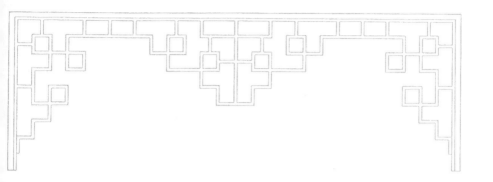

To Paradise

AMOY TO HAVANA
(1857)

There were other men like Chen Pan on the ship, not too young, but not too old either. From the farms, mostly, as far as he could tell. No weaklings. Cuba, the man in the Western suit had told him, needed sturdy workers. Chen Pan was taller than most of the recruits, and his arms were taut with muscles. His hair was tied back in a thick queue, but at twenty years old he barely needed to shave.

A few families came to see their men off. The women gave their husbands sticky rice balls and packets of seeds for their journey. There was no weeping. Even the smallest children were dry-eyed. Most of the men, like Chen Pan, went aboard alone and empty-handed.

That evening at sea, the coast of China gradually faded behind them. A haloed moon rose on a swell of wind, but this hopeful omen didn't alter the facts of the ship. It was outfitted like a prison, with irons and grates. The recruits were kept belowdecks, like animals in a pen. The shortest among them couldn't stand upright. Soon Chen Pan's neck ached from stooping.

Neither the British captain nor his crew spoke much Chinese. The captain issued his orders with a flat expression and a wave of his girlish hands. His crew was far more unruly. They threatened the recruits with muskets and cutlasses and rattan rods, shackled those whom the rods didn't tame. Chen Pan was struck with a hoisting rope for requesting an extra blanket.

Those men who'd brought food or tobacco on board began to barter and sell. These boiled chicken feet for your hemp sandals or your uncle's flute. A handful of pumpkin seeds for your stash of turnips or hard-boiled eggs. A day's opium for the woolen gloves. Gambling sprouted like snake-grass in every bunk. The incessant clicking of dice finely divided the hours. A man from W—— gathered most of the winnings and crowed, "If you were too dumb the life before, you won't be enlightened today!"

After his misfortunes in Amoy, Chen Pan refused to gamble. He guarded his Mexican coins, tucking them between the meager cheeks of his buttocks for safekeeping.

The men got beef jerky and rice gruel to eat. Chen Pan ate, although the taste of the food sickened him. It was oversalted, and the lack of adequate water made him desperately thirsty. Hour after hour, he thought more of his shoe-leather throat than of the life awaiting him in Cuba. Those who demanded more water were answered with blows. Chen Pan watched men drink their own urine, lick moisture from the walls of the ship. A few swallowed seawater until their stomachs swelled and they choked in their own filth.

A squat melon-grower from T—— announced that he would throw himself into the ocean to end his torment. Chen Pan crept on deck with two others to watch him jump. The melon-grower didn't shout or linger but simply stepped into the breeze. A moment later, the furling waves received him with indifference. The melon-grower had been an orphan and a bachelor. No destiny would be altered but his.

The ship continued to plow south into the hard-gusting wind. Chen Pan covered his ears so they wouldn't blow away altogether. He asked himself four questions: What was the last sound the melon-grower heard? The last color he saw before he died? How long would it take for the fish to devour him? Would this death complete his fate?

"Show me the person who doesn't die," shrugged a short-legged man next to Chen Pan.

This was something Chen Pan's father used to say, that death alone remained impartial. All the towering men, all the great beauties with kingfisher plumes in their hair—not a single one expected to grow old. But they, too, would return to dust. If it was true that man had two souls, one of the body and the other ethereal, then they would merge with the earth and the air after death.

Chen Pan knew that he didn't want to fade away slowly, like a dying candle—one day no different from the next; the dirt etched in his hands along with his fortunes. No, he would rather live in a blaze of courage and flame like Li Kuang, the ferocious warrior who'd battled the Huns, or the heroes in the stories his father had recounted to him.

Chen Pan's father had been as restless as these heroes, never reconciling himself to a life on their farm. He'd recited the Songs of Wu as he'd absent-mindedly hoed the wheat fields, grew devoted to the poetry of the deserted concubines of the Han court. He'd referred to the sun as the Lantern Dragon, the

Crow in Flight, the White Colt. The moon was the Silver Dish or the Golden Ring.

Father had taken the Imperial examinations for twenty years without success. He'd been a good poet but incapable of composing verses on assigned subjects, as was required by the examiners. He'd blamed his absorption of useless knowledge for overburdening his imagination. Before picking up his brush to write, he would rub his inkstick on a whetstone for a meditative hour as Chen Pan watched.

Chen Pan's mother ridiculed her husband as she hobbled from room to room on her lotus feet. "Ha! Everyone calls him a scholar, but he hasn't found a position yet. And in winter he wears a threadbare robe. This is how books fool us!" Chen Pan's mother was from a family of well-to-do farmers, and far from beautiful. She knew little poetry, but used to repeat the same line to nettle her improvident husband: *Poets mostly starve to death embracing empty mountains!*

After ten days of cramped, stinking squalor, a fight erupted belowdecks. A city man named Yang Yün, contrary as a donkey, shoved a quiet farmer out of his bunk. "Son of a whore!" the farmer shouted, punching Yang Yün in the chest. The city man pulled a knife from his vest and silvered the air with reckless slashing. The farmer disarmed him in no time, then promptly broke his nose.

Chen Pan watched the fight from behind his tattered book of poems, a last gift from his father. He decided that if Yang Yün or any of the other city cocks so much as jostled his elbow, he would knock them unconscious with a blow.

The captain's guards chained the troublemakers to iron posts. Others who'd cheered them on were flogged to intimidate the rest. When the stubborn Lin Chin resisted, the guards kicked him in the ribs until he spat blood. The next day he died and his body was dumped in the sea. It was said that Lin Chin didn't sink at first but floated alongside the ship for hours, his eyes fixed on the sky. Chen Pan wondered if the dead man's ghost would find its way back to China. Or would it wander forever among the unvirtuous and the depraved?

As the ship continued to sail, Chen Pan imagined his wife pounding the season's meager yield of grain in their yard, looking warily to the sky for rain. They'd been married for three years but had no children. Unlucky, despite what the matchmaker had predicted. On their wedding night, Chen Pan and his wife had drunk pomegranate wine and she'd grazed his chest with her soft, scant breasts. But month after month her womb spilled its blood.

Chen Pan's mother blamed his wife for ruining the family with her persistent barrenness. Weak and sallow-skinned, Mother ruled the farm from her bed, knees tucked to her chest, lotus feet curled and useless from the painful binding long ago. In her closet were three minuscule pairs of jeweled slippers, all that remained of a dowry once rich with silks and brocades.

She also chastised Chen Pan's younger brother for spending his days writing with his one brush and inkpot. "Even from the grave, your father has cursed you with his useless ways!" In winter, their house grew so cold that his small supply of ink froze.

On board, the recruits began to suffer every manner of illness. Cholera. Typhus. Dysentery. Bad luck, Chen Pan decided, had settled into every crevice of the ship. Nine men died the first month, not counting those killed in fights or beaten to death by the crew. Many more might have perished but for Chien Shih-kuang, sorcerer of herbs and roots. With his felt bag of magic, the wry herbalist from Z—— brewed teas to mend every imbalance, quieting fiery livers, warming cold organs, restoring the temperamental *ch'i*.

The captain had promised Chien Shih-kuang payment of passage back to Amoy in return for his services on board. The herbalist had agreed because he'd heard that in Cuba men knew the secret to halting the winter retreat of the sun. He, too, wished to learn this secret.

One night Chen Pan dreamed that bandits had set fire to his great-aunt's farm and that he alone was battling the flames. He woke up delirious, his skin hot and itchy. Chien Shih-kuang plastered a five-pointed leaf on Chen Pan's forehead with a few drops of a caustic liquid. When his fever broke, Chen Pan tried to pay the doctor with one of his precious Mexican coins, but Chien Shih-kuang refused it. (Years later, Chen Pan would learn that the herbalist had married a Spanish heiress in Avila and generously cured the poor.)

But not even Chien Shih-kuang could save the suicides. Chen Pan counted six altogether. After the melon-grower, another man jumped into the sea. One more poisoned himself with stolen opium. A boy, no older than fifteen, passed his days and nights in tears. He confided to Chen Pan that he was in great grief over having been decoyed on board. "I'm the only child of my parents!" he cried before thrusting a sharpened chopstick into his ear. In this way he stopped his regretting.

A native of K—— hanged himself with strips of torn clothing deep in the ship's hull. (The guards had beaten him savagely for siphoning rainwater from their private barrels.) Chen Pan thought his swaying sounded like the slow tearing of silk. With the winds stiff and the sea wide all around, he asked himself why someone would choose to die so confined and without air. Chen Pan wasn't certain what made a man ultimately want to live. He only knew that he would survive unless somebody managed to kill him.

The night the Wong brothers died, a squall engulfed the sea. The ship creaked and groaned like a sick man. The storm ripped off a mast and tossed two officers overboard. The men feared that the brothers' ghosts had cursed the ship, that they were causing the thunder and lightning, the wind from eight directions, the waves as high as the Buddha's temples. But by morning the sea was calm.

At noon, a pair of whales was spotted off the Cape of Good Hope. Chen Pan clambered to the deck to see the breaching beasts. "Maybe we should kill them and get some fresh meat," the lazy-eyed Wu Yao suggested. Chen Pan looked at him incredulously. It was obvious that this city boy had never caught so much as a pond carp.

The rumors spread with every day at sea. A bankrupt tailor pieced most of the gossip together, all the while quoting ancient sayings. *Caged birds miss their home forest. Pooled fish long for the deep.* Chen Pan listened closely to the tailor, but he didn't circulate the man's tidings: that their ship was headed for the Philippines; that every last man on board would be killed there, heart scooped from his chest; that they'd be sold to cannibals who savored yellow flesh.

There was talk of mutiny. Should they behead the captain and crew? Set fire to the vessel? Reverse their course to China? Chen Pan knew there were men on board fit for murder, experienced warriors who'd fought the British barbarians. Arrow-scarred, they'd been dragged from their prison cells to the ship. But the ones who talked loudest were most filled with hot air.

Chen Pan grew increasingly regretful. Had he deceived himself with his own grand dreams? How could he go home poorer than when he'd left? (Already, he imagined his mother's rebukes.) He tried to concentrate on his return to China a few years hence. A procession of men would follow him, triumphant in his sedan chair, carrying a hundred chests of princely gifts on their shoulders. Enough silk for three generations. New harnesses for the village horses. Countless jars of turtle eggs pickled in foreign wines. The villagers would gather around him, paying him the respect in life that his father had achieved only in death.

Because the days were long and the men so constricted, they entertained each other with stories about the tallest men who ever lived. Chung Lu-yüan, who was fond of lantern riddles, reported of a man who, sitting down, was as big as a mountain and could dam the course of a river with his ass. Hsieh Shuang-chi, a stevedore who was tricked on board by his greedy brother-in-law, told of a giant who drank a thousand gallons of celestial dew for his breakfast.

Chen Pan retold the jokes he'd learned from his beloved great-aunt. His favorite was the one about the evil warlord who'd had the length of his penis extended with a baby elephant's trunk. Everything went well for the warlord, Chen Pan said, until the day he passed a peanut vendor in the street.

There was also a dwarf on board who could imitate perfectly the sounds of a cassia-wood harp. His name was Yang Shi-fêng, and he sang of his land, where the tallest men grew to no more than three feet. In former times, he said, his countrymen had been sent as jesters and slaves to the Imperial Court. Then Yang Cheng came to govern the land of the dwarves and convinced the Emperor to annul his cruel trade. To this day every male born in T—— has Yang in his name.

Others recounted the tale of the impudent Monkey King. Entrusted with the job of guarding the Immortals' heavenly peaches, the Monkey King heartily partook of them instead. One transgression followed another, but none of the Jade Emperor's emissaries could catch the fearless simian. Finally, the Buddha himself cast a powerful spell that sealed the monkey under a mountain for five hundred years.

On a nearby bunk, a pig breeder from N—— reminded Chen Pan of his father. His hair fluttered with unruly tufts, no matter that the air was perfectly still. The pig breeder shared the last of his wife's pickled cabbage with Chen Pan. The taste made them both homesick. Chen Pan recalled the long summer afternoons his father had read poems to him, their plows left untouched in the shed. Before long the cicadas would sing, signaling the onset of autumn.

These lovely seasons and fragrant years falling
Lonely away—we share such emptiness here

When Chen Pan was thirteen, bandits had murdered his father for protesting the rape of the water-carrier's daughter. She was only ten, pretty and dull, and willingly had shown the bandits inside her neighbor's granary. Father's legend swelled and the villagers recounted his heroism, but Mother disputed their accolades. "What father leaves his children nothing but his good reputation to eat?" She scolded her sons to learn this lesson: "Avert your eyes to the sorrows of others and keep your own plates full!"

A fter three months at sea, Chen Pan's arms and legs grew soft and white as the flesh of the rich women he'd glimpsed in Amoy. Often he fantasized about these women, inhaled the scent of their lacquered hair, slowly dared to love them. He recalled the tales of the women of the old Imperial Court, who were protected by the Emperor's purple-robed eunuchs. Alluring women swathed in furs and jade, their gauze-silk sleeves blooming like orchids. Delicate women who drank only camel-pad broth and nibbled on rare winter fruit to maintain their complexions. Women best admired from afar, like the mountain mist.

Sometimes the men spoke wistfully of the roadside flowers who awaited them in Cuba, easy amber-colored whores who opened their legs for their own pleasure, expecting nothing in return. For all that it had cost him, Chen Pan couldn't remember his one night with the dancing girl in Amoy. There were only the memories of his mournful wife.

The ship passed through the Straits of Sunda without incident, then followed the verdant curve of Africa before veering west across the Atlantic. In St. Helena they stopped for fresh water, continuing on to Ascension, Cayenne, the Barbadian coast, and Trinidad. Chen Pan heard the crew announcing each port of call, but the longer he remained on board, the farther away Cuba seemed. Could his eight years of servitude have elapsed already?

When the ship finally reached Regla, across the bay from Havana, Chen Pan climbed to the top deck to get a better view. It was a hot, sunny morning, and the city looked like a fancy seashell in the distance, smooth pink and white. A brisk wind stirred the fronds of the palms. The water shone so blue it hurt his eyes to stare at it. When Chen Pan tried to stand on the dock, his legs slid out from under him. Others fell, too. Together, he and his shipmates looked like a spilled barrel of crabs.

The men were ordered to peel off their filthy rags and were given fresh clothes to present themselves to the Cubans. But there was no mistaking their wretchedness: bones jutted from their cheeks; sores cankered their flesh. Not even a strict regimen of foxglove could have improved their appearance. The recruits were rounded up in groups of sixty—wood haulers and barbers, shoemakers, fishermen, farmers—then parceled out in smaller groups to the waiting landowners.

A dozen Cubans on horseback, armed with whips, led the men like a herd of cattle to the *barracón* to be

sold. Inside, Chen Pan was forced to strip and be
examined for strength, like horses or oxen that were
for sale in the country districts of China. Chen Pan
burned red with shame, but he didn't complain. Here
he could no longer rely on the known ways. Who was
he now without his country?

One hundred fifty pesos was the going rate for a
healthy *chino*. A Spanish landowner paid two hundred for him, probably on account of his height. His
father had taught him that if you knew the name of a
demon, it had no power to harm you. Quickly, Chen
Pan asked one of the riders for the name of his buyer.
Don Urbano Bruzón de Peñalves. How would he ever
remember that?

Several landowners tried to cut off the queues of
their hires. Those who protested were beaten. Chen
Pan was relieved that his employer didn't insist upon
this. Now there was no question of his purpose in
Cuba. He was there to cut sugarcane. All of them
were. *Chinos. Asiáticos. Culís.* Later, there would be
other jobs working on the railroads or in the copper
mines of El Cobre, five hundred miles away. But for
now what the Cubans wanted most were strong backs
for their fields.

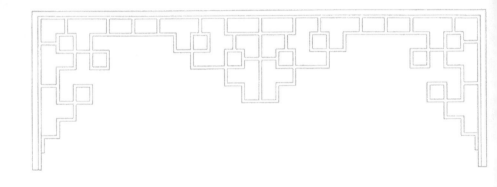

Vanishing Smoke

CENTRAL CUBA
(1857–1860)

Chen Pan arrived at La Amada plantation in time for the sugar harvest. He was thrown together with slaves from Africa, given a flat, straight blade to cut the sugarcane. The stalks were hard, like wood, but fibrous and tougher to chop. Clumps of dust shook loose in his face. Blisters sprouted like toadstools on his palms. Nets of iridescent flies settled on his skin as he worked, as he inhaled again and again the yellow-green fumes of the cane.

The heat began before dawn and persisted long after sundown. Chen Pan strained his back from all the bending. He tripped on lizards the width of his fist. A slip of his machete opened a wound in his shin that took many weeks to heal. The growing lines of oxcarts sagged under the weight of all the cane. Still, the work didn't stop.

The African slaves steadily slashed their rows of sugarcane. *Whoosh-whoosh-whack.* Three quick blows was all it took for them to strip the cane and leave an inch of stalk in the ground. Chen Pan had never seen men like this: Twice as wide as him, with thighs thick as oaks. Teeth that could grind his bones. Others as tall as two Chinese, with notched spines he could climb like a pine.

The Africans' skin seemed to darken the fields— reddish black skin or blue-black skin or skin brown as bark that gave off a smell of the woods. Most of the slaves had a spiderweb of scars on their backs, or strips of pink flesh still raw from the overseer's whip. Chen Pan watched a slave catch honeybees with his tongue, swallowing them like a bear. He claimed they didn't even sting.

The men came from places Chen Pan hadn't heard of: Mandinga, Arará, Carabalí. In China, no one would believe such men could exist.

From his first hour in the fields, it was clear to
Chen Pan that he was in Cuba not as a hired worker
but as a slave, no different from the Africans. That
he'd been tricked into signing his life away. At
night, his muscles burned with the day's work, but
he slept only fitfully. The same questions tormented
him. How would he ever return to his village? Build
the river house on stilts? Restore his father's good
name?

The slave quarters were a fetid honeycomb of
rotting wood—dirt and stink, rats and lice aplenty,
nothing freshly green. The air quivered with mosquitoes. Meager fires in the courtyard cooked sweet
potatoes, plantains, and malanga for dinner, giving
off sparks and a starch-violet smoke. Rooms were
filth holes with hard planks or hammocks for beds.
A miserable guard in a grillwork lookout had the only
key. The *mayoral* lived nearby with his fortress of
firearms.

A few old hags did the washing and cooking, tended
a dusty row or two of tubers. Chen Pan's shipmates
began growing their own vegetables from the seeds
they'd brought from home: bitter melon, squash, white
cabbage, eggplant, bok choy. One night, a chef from
Canton made a bird's nest soup so delicious it made
several men cry for their mothers.

After dark, no lights were permitted in the *bar-*

racón, so the slaves kept fireflies in tiny twig cages. Sometimes a homesick slave sang a song from his village, monotonous and sad, his words absorbed by the steady night-grinding of crickets. The restless ones spent hours pulling ticks from their skin. Men and women alike smoked cigars of wild tobacco to ward off evil. Because evil, they said, hung everywhere.

Talk was as rife as the vermin in the *barracón.* Chen Pan couldn't follow most of the stories, but what he understood, or thought he understood, unsettled him. Giant chameleons whose bite caused madness? Island snakes faster than full-trotting pigs? Scarlet vipers that turned themselves to hoops, tails in their mouths, and chased their victims to collapsing? The slaves spoke reverentially of a Yoruban girl who had bought her freedom by carving tortoiseshell combs. Everyone dreamed of this, to secure enough money to set himself free.

Sometimes an African hanged himself from the mahogany tree wearing his Sunday rags. The *bozales,* the newly arrived Africans, were especially prone to suicide. They threw themselves into the well or the boiling sugar cauldrons, swallowed mouthfuls of dirt, or suffocated themselves with their own tongues. On the plantation, there were many ways to die. The stuttering woodcutter from D—— hanged himself on the Africans' tree after a beating left him bent in two. Word spread on the plantation that even mild reprimands to *los chinos* could be disastrous to the master's investment.

At first, Chen Pan had trouble understanding anyone. Spanish sounded like so much noise to him. Firecrackers set off on New Year's Day. There was no bend in the sounds, no ups or downs, just *rat-tat-tat-tat-tat.* Like that. *Tra-ba-jo, tra-ba-jo.* He soon learned that he didn't need to know much more than that. Sometimes the Africans mixed in their own tribal languages. Abakuá. Lucumí.

Chen Pan liked the Africans. They showed him how to swing the machete, shared the yams they roasted in ashes. Cabeza de Piña, who could knock men senseless with a butt of his head, took an interest in Chen Pan and protected him like a brother. He called Chen Pan "Flecha," or arrow, on account of his long, straight spine. Cabeza said that Chen Pan, like him, was a son of the God of Fire.

In turn, Chen Pan taught his friend Chinese exercises to begin his day, to gather energy from the heavens to strengthen his body.

The other Chinese ridiculed Chen Pan. They said they wanted nothing to do with the Africans. They said the black men were liars, that they stank like monkeys and stole their food. But Chen Pan paid them no mind.

Everyone, Chinese and African alike, agreed on one thing: their hatred for the overseer, a burly pig of a criollo they called El Bigote for the mustache he wore like a door handle. Who did he imagine himself on that tired mare, his whip and pistol at the ready, his top boots muddy in the midday sun? Each time the master rode by to inspect the fields, El Bigote unctuously stammered: *"Sí, Señor. No, Señor. A sus órdenes, Señor."*

One day, El Bigote viciously whipped Chen Pan for telling one of his great-aunt's jokes (about a goatherd's first woman) that had made the men laugh so hard they dropped their machetes. "Baaaa-baaaa!" Chen Pan was still bleating when the lashes stripped the shirt off his back, leaving a lattice of blood. For many nights afterward, Chen Pan nursed his wounds with the Africans' healing leaves and planned his reprisal.

The flogging was not Chen Pan's last. For him and the other men, the whip cracked for any small wrong— if they slowed down or spoke their own language or dared to protest. Twenty lashes for outright defiance. Thirty more if the offender persisted. After that, it was the shackles for two months or working fettered in the fields.

For Chen Pan, the silence was worse than the sting of the whip. He felt his unspoken words festering inside him, ordinary words like "sun" and "face" and "tree." Or snatches of poems he longed to shout out loud, like the one about Lady Xi. Hundreds of years ago—Chen Pan heard his father's voice reciting it— the King of Chu defeated the Ruler of Xi and took his wife in the spoils of war.

> *No present royal favour could efface*
> *The memory of the love that once she knew*
> *Seeing a flower filled her eyes with tears*
> *She did not speak a word to the King of Chu*

Now and then a breeze blew through the sugarcane fields, carrying a scent of jasmine or heliotrope. This heartened Chen Pan. No matter that he was stuck on this devil island surrounded by mangroves and flesh-hungry sharks, that his arm often dropped in mid-swing from pure exhaustion. He imagined the breezes as fresh breaths from the sea, coaxing boats along the horizon, their sails puffed up and purposeful.

Sometimes he distracted himself by spying on the few female slaves in the fields. On lucky Sundays, Chen Pan watched the younger ones bathing in the stream or lying with their lovers in the thickets. He noticed with longing that in the heat of love they didn't close their eyes or turn their heads.

The fights over the women grew so bloody and bitter that someone usually ended up dead. *As long as bones are rare, a pack of dogs can't share.* Three slaves came to blows over a plump girl who worked in the kitchen. The two smaller men managed to strangle the bigger one, then bashed in his head. At the funeral the slaves chanted and clapped over the lifeless body, clamoring for the dead man's safe passage to Africa. Then they sealed his eyes shut with semen before burying him in the woods.

On weekends, fiestas animated the *barracón*. The criollo trader came around with his white bread and fritters. He also sold calicoes and muslins, peanut candies, muscle ointments, and gingham handkerchiefs. An occasional cockfight heightened the excitement. Chen Pan used to play the cocks in China, sneaking off to W—— after his mother and wife were asleep. He liked to judge a rooster by its battle-trim, by the ferocity in its eyes. Once, he'd bought a new hoe with his winnings.

There were other entertainments. Slave games over whose prick was biggest. Many such contests. In one, the men thrust their *pingas* through a hole in a deep wooden box with ashes at the bottom. The man who pulled his *pinga* out with the most ash was pronounced the winner. Cabeza de Piña frequently won this game.

When Cabeza was ordered to sleep in the stocks for fighting with the *mayoral*, several Africans surrounded Chen Pan. They accused him of getting Cabeza in trouble. But Chen Pan fought back. No other Chinese bothered to speak to the slaves, he complained, so why were they attacking him? When the Africans forced Chen Pan to put his *pinga* in the ashes box, he wanted to vanish from the shame. He pulled it out, shriveled, with no ash at all.

B y harvest's end, Chen Pan was hacking his way through the fields with the same proficiency he'd first admired in the Africans. As the last of the cane matured, its skin grew brittle, its stems clotted with treacly juice. Chen Pan learned to move to the rhythm of the swaying stalks, to the heat and buzz of the insects. He cut cane until time lost all meaning, until his throat cracked drought-dry, until his dreams blew nothing but dust.

If he completed his contract in Cuba, what would he have to show for it? No money and an old-man body. His fate burnt in the fields. A dead-dog luck.

In the last grueling weeks of the *zafra,* the sugar mill bell tolled twenty times in a single workday. Chen Pan's life was metered by the *snap-crack* punctuations of the whip, by his sun-cured skin torn off in strips. A few of the *chinos* got less arduous jobs. They loaded the cane onto the crushing machines or tended the boiling sap. Chen Pan was picked for these jobs, too. But after the suffocation of ship and *barracón,* he couldn't bear to stay indoors for long. The sun was brutal, it was true, but sometimes cranes flew overhead, rinsing him with their shadows and wandering luck.

A cloud-crane setting out, you'd rather
go back home, white clouds and beyond,
sip streamwater, sleep in empty valleys . . .

Chen Pan missed his great-aunt most of all. Before going to Amoy, he'd taken leave of her under the eaves of her thatch-roofed house. How he'd loved the neat rows of her chrysanthemums. They'd spent hours collecting mulberry leaves, and her blackened teeth had flashed whenever she'd told him a ribald joke. As a child, Chen Pan had believed that his penis (and every other boy's, for that matter) was little more than a source of mirth for women.

"Remember, we own nothing in death," his great-aunt had said, embracing him. "Go safely and return home."

Chen Pan's father often had auditioned his poems for this beloved aunt. She was old and unschooled, but she listened to her nephew attentively. Whenever Father read her an expression she didn't understand, he would scratch out the line. He'd decided to write only what any good peasant could appreciate.

Chen Pan composed letters to his family in his head.

Dear Auntie. Dear Wife. Dear Brother. I am not dead.
But he didn't finish these letters. Better to let everyone
think that brigands had robbed and killed him, that
vultures had come and plucked out his eyes. He knew
that his wife would burn incense in his name, urging
his ghost home. Chen Pan liked to imagine her surprise at his return. But with each swing of his machete,
that prospect grew more and more remote.

Sometimes a storm broke the monotony of the days,
but soon the downpours became predictable: the clouds
built their same gray cliffs every afternoon, the rains
lasted no more than an hour. And at dusk, the fields
grew tremulous with fireflies. Only a calamity made
one day different from the rest. Like the time Yeh Nien
got struck by lightning as he raised his machete in a
storm, or the morning slow-witted Eulice lost three
toes to a toppled ox.

Late one afternoon, a magnificent thundershower
obscured the fields. The slaves couldn't see to the
ends of their machetes, but they were forced to keep
cutting cane just the same. In the blurring confusion,
Chen Pan caught sight of El Bigote shouting orders at
a field boss. He picked up a sharp stone, aimed carefully, then hurled it at the overseer's temple—the
very spot, Chen Pan knew, that if hit correctly would
instantly kill a man.

Every slave was whipped in retribution for El Bigote's murder, but nobody confessed to the crime or to

having witnessed it. No one said a word to Chen Pan either, but the slaves offered him small tributes. He got his pick of the machetes at dawn and was permitted to drink first from the noontime water trough. *Akuá mbori boroki ñangué,* the Africans murmured. The goat is castrated only once.

Years before, a traveling acrobat had come to Chen Pan's village with an enormous macaque monkey on a leash. It was summer and the macaque broke loose and climbed his family's kumquat tree, gorging, uninvited, on the fruit. No amount of coaxing could get the monkey down. Then it tried to mount all the local dogs, including the little helpless ones like his great-aunt's Pekingese. Chen Pan had killed that monkey, too, with a single throw of a stone.

The women took more notice of Chen Pan after he'd killed El Bigote. A skinny slave named Rita started coming around to his end of the *barracón.* Her skin was smooth and mauve-looking, her legs stick-straight. When she walked toward him, her narrow hips shifting rhythmically, Chen Pan felt his whole body grow taut with ardor. Rita confessed to Chen Pan that he tempted her curiosity.

"Chinito lindo, chinito lindo," she chimed, running her fingers down his arms.

The other men hooted and teased Chen Pan. He began dreaming of Rita, of her voice sifting through his loosened hair, of her lips hungrily parting to receive his kiss. In the mornings, he awoke with Rita simmering under his skin.

Chen Pan thought of his wife waiting for him on their wheat farm, her thin hair tied in a topknot. She wasn't a bad woman. She'd cooked for him, mended his clothes, lain with him when he'd asked her to, even in the high heat of noon. Chen Pan hadn't loved her. He knew this now. When they'd separated beneath the willow tree wreathed with a rotten vine, he'd felt nothing.

A few days later, Chen Pan presented Rita with a pocket mirror he'd bought from the criollo trader. "Now you will have to admit how beautiful you are and forgive me the passion I feel for you." Chen Pan had practiced saying this to himself in his halting Spanish. Rita angled the mirror to catch the sunlight and examined herself full in the face. She seemed pleased by her reflection.

"Do you love me?" Rita asked in her singsong voice.

"Sí," Chen Pan said, lowering his head.

The same day, Chen Pan noticed the master eyeing Rita. Don Urbano lingered by her patch of sugarcane. He had her machete specially sharpened and sent an indoor slave to serve her fresh mamey juice in the shade. After dinner he ordered Rita's steady lover,

Narciso, to be switched to the night shift at the mill. Then the master summoned Rita to his bed.

When Narciso returned from work the next morning, the *mayoral,* without a word of warning, shot him dead. Nobody was allowed to bury him. Instead he was fed to the bloodhounds before the entire *barracón,* piece by bloody piece. Poor Mandingo spirit, the slaves chanted, lost and forever wandering. How the old hags clucked: *Gallina negra va pone' huevo blanco.* Black hen gonna lay a white egg.

As Rita's belly swelled, the rest of her grew leaner, as if by a transference of flesh. She forgot Chen Pan and her friends in the *barracón,* forgot her own name and the gift of the little mirror, forgot that she was a slave. Every night Chen Pan knelt by her hammock, whispering in her ear. He told her the story of the herd boy and the weaving maid, who were turned into stars by the girl's celestial mother and placed on opposite sides of the Milky Way. Only one night a year, on the seventh night of the seventh moon, could they meet.

The other Chinese said Chen Pan was crazy, in love with a dead girl. The Africans also believed this, but they were too tender-mouthed to say it aloud.

It became clear to the new overseer that Rita was of no more use in the fields. Within a few weeks, she was sold to a coffee plantation in the mountains of Oriente. Everyone said that to pick coffee in the rain would finish off a slave in half the time of sugar-cane. La Gorda, the Bantu witch, threw her divining cowries and predicted that Rita would not work in the fields again: *She will die upon reaching her destination, choking the boy-ghost in her womb.*

After the cane was cut and ground, the days were taken with lesser tasks—repairing tools, weeding the dormant fields, reseeding them in the intervals between the rains. A few Chinese adopted Spanish names, cut off their queues, adapted their palates to the local food. They took the names of wealthy Cubans, hoping for their same prosperity. Yü Ming-hsing became Estéban Sariñana. Li Chao-ch'un renamed himself Perfecto Díaz and slicked his hair back with perfumed grease. Thickheaded Kuo Chan insisted on being called Juan-Juan Capote.

"Why Juan-Juan?" Chen Pan asked him.

"Twice as much luck," he replied.

Kuo Chan learned to dance as well as the Africans, learned to move his hips to the drums. He forgot he was a *chino* at all.

Chen Pan's grief over Rita made him lucky in gambling. His opponents said that Chen Pan won time and again because he didn't care if he lost. Distraction, they said, was what he sought. The Chinese and Africans played their games heatedly—*botón, fanfän, chiffa*. Chen Pan was lucky but not greedy. He stopped playing after winning five or six pesos. No use winning more and losing all, he decided. Dead men—yellow, black, or white—had no friends.

On New Year's Day, twelve Chinese escaped La Amada plantation. Chen Pan was angry that he hadn't been included in their plans until all but one of the men were hunted down and stock-shackled for ten days. As a warning, Chen Pan and the other *chinos* were forced to watch as the fugitives had fingers chopped off from their weaker hands. Then they were thrown back into the fields to cut more sugarcane.

For months afterward, all anyone talked about was the *chino* who got away: Tiao Mu, the fisherman from F——. It was said that Tiao Mu had jumped into the river with the bloodhounds upon him and disappeared. Vanishing Smoke, everyone called him. The first Chinese *cimarrón*.

The Africans claimed that Ochún had protected Tiao Mu, that the river goddess had turned him to mist before sweeping him off to the safety of her sister, Yemayá, who ruled the blue seas. Tiao Mu, they said, must offer Ochún honey and gold for the rest of his days to stay well protected. Would he know, the slaves debated, what to do?

Nobody ever heard from Tiao Mu again, but no one doubted that he was alive and free. Everyone on the plantation thought more highly of the Chinese on account of Tiao Mu. After he escaped, *los chinos* were treated with more respect.

In May, Chen Pan slipped away from the other slaves during a march to weed a distant field. He held his breath and sank to his knees in the tall grasses. The crickets screeched his fear, but nobody noticed that he was missing. Crows squawked and taunted from a nearby ceiba tree. Chen Pan remembered what Cabeza had told him: the tree was their mother; her sap, blood; her touch, a tender caress.

There were mounds of dirt beneath the ceiba, talismans buried amid the roots. Chen Pan crawled to the tree and rubbed its sacred earth on his face and throat, on his temples to clear his thinking. It was moist and acrid and cooled him, steadied his jumping blood. Immense sulfur-colored butterflies hovered in the tree's lowest branches. A contrary wind stirred its leaves.

Chen Pan stood up and walked away. Too easy, he suspected. How could elation eclipse despair in one fell swoop? In the woods, every rustle and hiss frayed his nerves. How had this happened? He'd come to Cuba to seek his fortune and now he would end up peeling bark for his supper. But what time was there for lamenting? To survive, Chen Pan decided, he would first need to steal a knife.

By midnight, alone in the forest, Chen Pan sat high in another ceiba tree, willing himself invisible. Bloodhounds barked madly in the distance, searching for him, devil ghosts in their throats. The wind carried their news like ten thousand swollen tongues. The Africans had spoken of the restless demons that roamed the island's woods, disguised in animal furs. High in the ceiba tree, his guts grinding, Chen Pan prepared for the worst.

There was no moon that first night and for many nights afterward, only the mimicking birds, scattering spirits, the trogons hiccuping in the canopy of trees. The owls were the worst, shrieking at him in Chinese. One owl—tattered and brown and without markings—followed him for nine months.

"Unfilial son!" it scolded again and again.

Chen Pan concluded that his mother had died and her ghost had come to haunt him—for running away from China, for not sending her money or producing a grandson. He tried to explain to her why he'd left Amoy, that he'd planned to return to their village and make them all rich. But she wouldn't listen.

He stole eggs from a tenant farmer to appease his mother's spirit. He offered her tender meat he'd smoked over a fire—an unborn *almiquí* he'd torn from its mother's slit belly, the bones delicate as flower stems. He made her a wreath from palm fronds and jungle orchids, more beautiful than any in China, gave her wild pineapples and pomegranates oozing a ruby juice.

"Eat," Chen Pan begged her. "These are better than our peaches, juicier than the Emperor's plums."

"Unfilial son!" she screeched back.

He brewed teas from sweet leaves to ease her misery, prepared a bed of guinea grass and reeds by a clear stream for her to rest, roasted doves with wild taro and honey he'd scooped from hidden hives. When it rained so hard the forest seemed a swamp and it was impossible to start a fire, Chen Pan built his mother a shelter of lopped branches and palm-tree leaves and bound it with *majagua,* a natural twine.

"Unfilial son!"

Mostly, Chen Pan walked and walked until his feet bled, following streams and the slow rotation of stars. He grew tired, careless, twisted his ankle in a clump of vines. When his mouth got infected, he packed moss on his gums to keep them pink. He lost one tooth anyway, a molar so black and angry with pain that he had to yank it out with a liana vine.

His own shadow grew unfamiliar to him, thin and strangely angled. He suspected that his great-aunt had died, too. Now only his wife and his brother were left on the farm. In China it was said that owl chicks ate their mothers as soon as they were big enough to fly. Perhaps he could hunt this tormenting bird, cook

it, devour it once and for all. How else to get rid of it?
At the thought, Chen Pan began to tremble.

That night the owl's maternal scourge stopped
without warning. The forest turned cemetery-quiet.
Moonlight unsettled the trees. Birds flew overhead
soundlessly. This was much worse than his mother's
scoldings, Chen Pan thought. At dawn he slept a little, dreamed of lotuses and speeding geese.

Chen Pan trudged through the woods, his heart
knocking hollow-loud. His footsteps echoed in the
leaves before they fell, shivering, from the trees. He
ate only wild guavas. Shit a pink stream. His skin
turned as red-brown as the island earth. Chen Pan
saw smoke rising from behind a cluster of palm trees.
He heard the sound of coughing. Were there other
cimarrones in the forest, hiding like him? Should he
turn himself in? Go back to cutting sugarcane? Of
what use was his freedom now?

He remembered something his father had told him.
It is in death alone that we return home. So Chen Pan
arranged a bed of cobwebs and silvery leaves on the
bat guano that cushioned the floor of a limestone
cave, smeared pollen on his face and hands. He would
die there, leave his bones to crumble. He would die
there in that nowhere cave, and then his ghost would
fly home to China.

The next morning Chen Pan awoke feeling rested.
The air was damp and the sky clear. Above him, lum-

bering high along a branch of a cedar tree, was a fat *jutía*. If he succeeded in killing it, Chen Pan decided, he would remain in Cuba. He picked up a speckled stone and threw it with all his strength. The rodent seemed to hover in midair before collapsing to the ground. It would make an excellent breakfast.

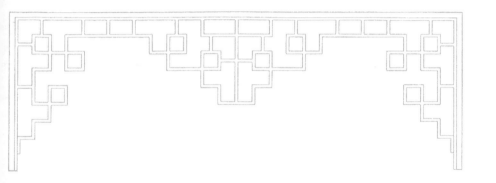

North

NEW YORK CITY

(1968)

omingo Chen was startled again by the fat floating egg of the moon. Nobody at work mentioned how it stayed elliptically full all summer, not even Félix Puleo, who kept an extra mattress on the rooftop of his building for his secondary girls and had, one might say, a fine view of heaven. So how could the moon stay full all summer long and nobody notice?

There'd been nothing in the news about celestial

aberrations. Domingo would've heard about it because there was always a radio pumping, around the clock. At the Havana Dragon, the music rumba-plena-merengued all night, ricocheted off the moon and bounced back to fry cutlets. And when the music wasn't playing, the bad news was blaring—subway decapitations and hijackings to Cuba and all the tragic static of Vietnam.

Domingo stuck his head out of the kitchen's back door for relief from the steaming dishes. Tonight Venus was in her usual yellow nest, and Mars still reigned as god of war. Even with the freakish moon and the miserable ration of stars, the view of the sky comforted him. His mother used to compare the planets to the *santos*. Venus was Ochún. Mars was Changó. And Saturn with all its rings of knowledge was the serene Obatalá.

It hadn't been easy since he and his father had left Cuba last winter. Those first November weeks, Domingo could've sworn that someone had put the sun in cold storage, that the wind was blowing inside him—he'd never been so frozen in his life. And his father had gotten thin enough to seem to be vanishing altogether. Then both of them had come down with the flu and didn't leave their apartment for days. They'd spent Christmas Eve collapsed on their salvaged-from-the-street sofa, wrapped in towels, a searing ache in their bones.

But now it was summer, and New York was far more hospitable. Domingo loved roaming the city on his days off—along its slate-colored rivers, beneath its granite towers, down its neon-loud avenues—watching the women. Manhattan was a glorious *jardín de mujeres*. Brown girls. Pink girls. White and yellow girls in every soft-fleshed shape and size. When the sun was out, they were everywhere in their skimpy dresses (some made of *disposable* paper!). They wore white vinyl go-go boots and armfuls of plastic bangles and frosted lipstick that reminded him of the coconut ice cream cones he'd loved in Guantánamo.

Domingo rated the fountain at Lincoln Center as his top lookout. At lunchtime, he'd settle there with a hot dog and a potato knish (just like a square croquette, he thought) and follow the high-ribbed ballerinas hurrying across the plaza. In his own neighborhood, there were dozens of women to consider. The unkempt Barnard girls with their nice teeth and unfettered breasts. The big-bottomed waitress on 108th Street who let the college boys feel her up for the price of a Sprite. The Puerto Rican *mamitas* on Amsterdam Avenue.

The dishwasher broke down in the middle of the dinner rush, and so Domingo had to wash everything by hand. He couldn't work fast enough to please the waiters, irascible old Chinese men like his father who'd left Cuba after the Revolution. *"¡Mas platos! ¡Mas cubiertos!"* Domingo scraped and rinsed plate after plate of house specials—breaded steak with onions, fried rice, and *tostones*—until his stomach flip-flopped with disgust.

After work, he headed downtown to see Ray Barretto's late show at the Village Gate. Domingo knew it drove his father crazy that he spent all his money on concerts and clothes. But what was he supposed to do? Save for his retirement? Of course, he'd bought one of those cool knit shirts everyone was wearing and blue-tinted sunglasses to match. When he'd put it together to show his father, Papi had just stared back at him from his chopping block.

"But Papi, it's El Watusi Man!" Domingo had whined. How could anyone put a price on that? But his father kept chop-chopping his cabbage in silence. Papi was preparing stir-fried cabbage with dried shrimp. He'd soaked the shrimp in boiling water before dropping them into the smoking wok. They popped and sizzled when they hit the oil, filling the apartment with a sharp ocean scent.

The nightclub was jammed, but Domingo talked himself into a seat up front, next to a washed-out little nurse with a mole on her cheek. El Watusi Man was hitting the skins like a dialect freaked by thunder. Smoke-sounding *rumbero. De otro mundo.* Domingo felt the *timba* as if the Man were playing his own bones. *Ashé olu batá.* He closed his eyes and let loose, felt the groove, a deep reverie, the pulse of his own peculiar birth.

"Hey, where you from?" the nurse asked him when the music finally stopped.

Domingo wanted to answer her, to say that his blood was a mix of this and that. So how was he supposed to choose who he wanted to be?

"Cuba," he said. "I'm from Cuba."

Then Domingo followed the little nurse to her apartment in Chinatown and made love to her on her dead mother's bed (doilies scattered everywhere like desiccated snowflakes). The nurse told him that she usually dated only white men but she'd make an exception in his case. Domingo knew then that he couldn't love the little nurse, but he still felt tenderly toward her.

It was dark when Domingo left the nurse's apartment. A faint drizzle coated the last rim of night. Already, Chinatown was coming to life with vendors and bargaining customers. The fog from the river seemed to remold everything. A mist-veiled widow became a scurrying bride. A dangling row of red-roasted chickens saluted each passerby. And everywhere he went, frantic little dogs barked messages from the dead.

On Mott Street, garbage lined the streets like wildflowers. A crack in the sidewalk mimicked the curve of a maple branch. The Wall Street skyscrapers loomed arrogantly to the south. At a cutlery shop, dozens of knives were on display: pocketknives encased in red enamel, serrated ones for cutting bread, carving knives and meat cleavers and in the back row, six subtly carved daggers inlaid with bone.

In front of a seafood shop, a broom-thin woman was objecting to the inhumane treatment of amphibians. Turtles chopped and decarapaced alive. Pitiable frogs in overcrowded tanks. The protester shouted, stirring the fog with her placard. Behind her, long rows of lobsters lay dully on mounds of crushed ice, their claws held shut by rubber bands.

Around the corner Domingo found a cafeteria that served dumplings for breakfast. The waiter said that he could read the future in the pinch and tuck of the dumplings' folds, lucky numbers for that week's lottery. "Just fifty cents extra," he said. But Domingo politely declined.

The hot tea burned through him. He lowered his face over the steaming cup, then watched as vaporous bits of his features beaded on the low-slung ceiling. He poured sugar directly into the pot. It dissolved easily. To work the sugarcane fields, his father had told him, was to go wooing mournful ghosts. The chain gangs of runaway souls, ankles ulcerated and iron-eaten and wrapped in rags. Or the luckier suicide ghosts who'd killed themselves dressed in their Sunday best.

Domingo poked the shrimp dumplings with his chopsticks. There were no obvious messages for him, at least none that he could see. The dumplings were hot and juicy with just enough scallions.

Outside the cafeteria, everything seemed to be falling, washed away by the morning rain. Domingo tasted the salt in the air, the pyramids of ginger and stacks of watercress, the seared flesh of the ducks in their rotisseries. He recalled how after every rainstorm, snails had appeared like jewels in their garden in Guantánamo, snails in iridescent colors and rainbow stripes. They were so beautiful they should have been toxic, but in fact they were quite delicious. He and his father had collected the snails, gently tugging them off leaves or the trunks of palm trees. Stir-fried snails with sugar peas was one of Papi's specialties.

It was only seven o'clock, but dozens of people streamed past Domingo. He made his way to the subway station on Canal Street. A blind man was climbing the steps and counting—eighteen, nineteen, twenty—as Domingo descended. A gust of warm air swept up from the station. The platform was noisy with Chinese schoolchildren in starched blue smocks. They were on their way to the zoo, Domingo overheard one of them say.

Before the Revolution, his father had taken him to the traveling circus in Santiago de Cuba to see the foreign curiosities: the American monster horse, the incredible Gorilla Boy, the Erudite Pig from London. The pig, Domingo remembered, had held a dictionary between its hooves while solemnly nodding its head.

The light from a bare bulb was terribly bright. Domingo felt a pain in his eyes, like the times he'd stared too long at the sun as a child. He heard the electricity ticking in the thick wires of the station, doing its invisible math. Sparks flew from the wheels of the train on the opposite tracks. Then his own train pulled in.

A half hour later, Domingo got off at 110th Street and walked to the Cathedral of Saint John the Divine. There were scaffolds everywhere. Men in overalls were repairing the ceiling and the Gothic turrets. Domingo dipped three fingers in the marble basin of holy water and crossed himself twice. It was confusing inside, the light distorted by the vast expanses of stained glass.

Near the front of the cathedral, to the right of the altar, was an alcove for the Virgin Mary. Long-stemmed roses were wilting on a bed of ferns at her feet. Domingo sat in the third pew and brought his hands together. He wanted to pray, but he wasn't sure what to ask. Mamá had told him once that the

Virgin was partial to ascetics, outcasts, and forgotten men but that she would take on lesser cases if pressed.

Domingo stared at the Virgin and wondered whether she ever longed to join the everyday fray of the ordinary. Were transcendent beings even capable of envy? Maybe on earth she would go bad—hold up convenience stores, steal packets of sugar-powdered doughnuts for the road. Or gang up with her sisters and form a posse of murderous virgins from Guadalupe, Lourdes, Regla (La Virgen de Regla was certainly a looker in black and blue). *¿Y por qué no?* Domingo imagined them in leather jackets and wraparound shades, boots to there, crows on their shoulders instead of the Holy Ghost.

He lowered his head guiltily, half expecting to see a cadre of outraged saints marching over to show him the door. Then he stole another glance at the Virgin. He noticed her left foot crushing the head of a hideous snake, presumably Satan. Her toes were plump and painted red. He wanted to suck them.

Domingo thought of the time his older stepsister had fondled him on a visit to Guantánamo. Mariana Quiñones still played the harp for the Municipal Orchestra of Oriente. With her plink-plinky voice and her calloused fingertips, she'd expertly coaxed Domingo's *pinguita* from his short pants. He was only eight, but he'd sworn to Mariana that he knew how to keep a secret.

Domingo's building was only a few blocks away. He climbed the four flights to his and his father's apartment. The walls of the stairwell were painted a dirty internal pink. There was a stench of meat in the hallway. No doubt that vet down the hall was pan-frying his weekly supply of beef. The vet said he'd eaten nothing but hamburgers since he'd returned from Vietnam, 100 percent USDA.

There were other vets in the neighborhood. Thin howls of men who spooked anyone who looked their way. Crispulo "Crispy" Morán came back from Danang missing both legs and a chunk of his skull that he tried to hide with an old bebop hat. Domingo wondered whether Crispy still had his balls, but he didn't have the nerve to ask him. Crispy liked to shoot pigeons in Morningside Park, then stuff them with his *mami*'s yellow rice. Sometimes he snorted cocaine off the edge of his wheelchair until his brains were fried and all he could say was, *The sky there is fuckin' bigger than here.*

Papi had left early for his job at the ice factory in the Bronx. He would be angry with Domingo for making him worry. But Domingo was tired of having to take care of his father. Papi refused to buy groceries or wash his clothes, and he needed constant reminding to take his pills.

Domingo showered with the almond soap Mamá had given him before he'd left Cuba. The hot steam concentrated its scent. He remembered the boleros she'd listened to while delivering babies, the rum she'd drunk in the same green tumbler night after night. In the mornings, Mamá would be in a sour mood and she would reach for a shoe or the stout black umbrella to teach Domingo a lesson. He'd never understood for what.

Domingo changed into his uniform for his early shift at the Havana Dragon. He liked how his name was embroidered on his shirt in red script, clean and raised as a fresh scrape (just another affectation, Papi had sniffed). Domingo combed his hair straight back, no part, and clipped his fingernails. Then he wrote his father a note and left it on the kitchen table. He double-locked the front door and raced down the stairs, taking care not to touch the grimy, swaying banister. He was ten minutes late for work.

His boss was waiting for him at the restaurant. Guiomar Liu had been in New York for thirty years, but Domingo, after nine months, spoke better English. Domingo took ESL classes at a public high school twice a week. He was particularly fond of English verbs, the way they lined up regularly as sheep. His teacher, Miss Gilbert, said

Domingo gave English an unusual cadence. He'd add a brush of the guiro here, the *pa-pa-pá* of the bongos there, the happy clatter of timbales.

Languages you acquired, Domingo decided, didn't have the same memory-packed punch as the mother tongue. But did you have to dissolve one language to accommodate another? Back home, Domingo had wanted to study marine biology. He'd known the names and habits of every fish and mollusk, crustacean and sponge for miles around. Of what use was any of it here?

Last month, Liu had begun opening the Havana Dragon for breakfast. He'd plastered the windows with hand-lettered signs: two eggs with ham and coffee, ninety-nine cents; a Spanish omelet with roasted peppers, a dollar more; pancakes and bacon with a free glass of buttermilk. But business remained slow. When Domingo was a boy, he'd chosen foods more for their texture than their taste. Slippery foods were the best: avocados, tomatoes, spaghetti with butter. Maybe one day he would open his own place and serve nothing but oysters.

His father had worked for seventeen years as a short-order cook at the American naval base in Guantánamo. Once a year he used to bring Domingo to work, usually on the Fourth of July. The Americans had looked gargantuan to him, another species altogether. Still, he'd liked their uniforms and their parades and the chocolate-filled lollipops everyone gave him. At the PX, Domingo had been impressed by the walls lined floor to ceiling with cans of peaches in heavy syrup.

On weekends Papi had brought home sirloin steaks, buckets of mashed potatoes, and buttered peas from the officers' events. Domingo used to wait for his father on the porch of their whitewashed cement house off Parque Martí, rubbing a lucky fish vertebra in his pocket. That was before the Revolution. Afterward, Mamá refused to eat any of the Yankees' food—even when Papi donned his chef's hat and grilled cheeseburgers for Domingo's tenth-birthday party. Domingo often fell asleep to his parents' bitter arguing.

When revolutionary officials had ordered his father to give up his job with the Americans, Papi had refused. Working the grill had made him a traitor? No amount of haranguing from the Committee for the Defense of the Revolution could convince him of that.

On his afternoon break, Domingo took a walk along the Hudson River. The sky was low and dark with clouds. Lush smells seeped up from the soil, stung with unexpected perfumes. He watched as two sailboats glided by in opposite directions. Domingo had used his father's contacts at the

U.S. naval base to get Papi and himself out of Cuba. Finally, they'd left the island behind like a rainy season. But what was their world now? What belonged to them? Was it possible, Domingo wondered, to be saved and destroyed at once?

He wasn't sure that he regretted leaving Cuba, but he still missed it, including its more ludicrous thefts. Last year, his Tío Eutemio had been forced to give up his congas. The authorities in Guantánamo had decided that the drums were cultural artifacts because they'd once belonged to Domingo's great uncle, the legendary El Tumbador. Now the congas were on display at a folklore museum where *el pueblo* could admire them but never hear their *boom-tak-tak-a-tak* again.

On Domingo's mother's side, most of the men were *congueros* and *batá* drummers from way back. In Cuba, the name Quiñones was synonymous with rhythm. His uncles and cousins were in demand for the *toques,* holy ceremonies that coaxed the gods down from heaven. When their drums started talking, all available deities would stop their celestial bickering and drop in for dancing and good times.

Domingo had no aptitude to play, but he was an ardent listener. In Guantánamo, the drums were everywhere: on street corners and in carnival bands, at parties and *fiestas de santos. Kimpá, kimpá, kimpá.* His mother said that drumming was for blacks who didn't work and drank too much, meaning, of course, her brothers and uncles. But Domingo paid her no mind. *Tinkitín, tinkitín.* When he listened to the drums, he felt right in his own skin.

Business picked up at dinnertime. A crowd of customers rushed in to the Havana Dragon after a movie let out down the block. It was raining and people shook themselves dry like dogs. The humidity steamed up the windows. Pinkish bolts of lightning lit up the sky. Domingo loved lightning, especially when he woke up to it in the middle of the night. It reassured him to know that nature soldiered on while he slept.

After the storm subsided, a famous trumpeter dropped in for *cafesito* and a slice of pound cake à la mode. The man had fronted one of the best bands on the island until he'd defected in 1962. The trumpeter was wearing a shabby suit and a woolen cap pulled low on his forehead. His fingers were long and translucent. Ash from three cigarettes slowly collected on his plate.

Que te importa que te amé
Si tú no me quieres ya?
El amor que ha pasado
No se debe recordar . . .

At eight-thirty, two policemen walked into the Havana Dragon looking for Domingo. He watched them confer with Liu before they moved toward the kitchen. The shorter one took off his cap. His hair was flaming red and cut so short it stood on end. The sound of him cracking his knuckles gave him even more of an electrical air. The policeman said that Domingo's father had jumped off a subway platform on Jerome Avenue in the Bronx. A dozen people had seen him jump, including the conductor of the #4 train. There were two bruises on his head, not much left to the rest of him. Could Domingo accompany them to the morgue to identify his father's remains?

Domingo felt every nerve in his body converge in his throat. He wanted to say something, but all he could think of was the questions he used to ask Papi as a kid, the ones that had made his father laugh and shake his head. *What does distance look like? Who discovered time? What is sound made of? Does everyone feel pain the same?*

His father had been alive yesterday, Domingo thought. In the morning Papi had shuffled toward the subway station on Broadway, his lobster fists in children's mittens, his thick-socked feet stuffed into cheap canvas shoes. He'd returned home that afternoon, his hands chapped scarlet, his body shrunken. He'd made stir-fried cabbage with dried shrimp for dinner. Before Domingo had left for the late shift, he'd undressed his father for bed like a baby.

Outside, the street looked smoky and distorted after the rain. The diseased oak in front of the restaurant was gone. Last week, men in blue jumpsuits had come with their helmets and electric saws and methodically dismembered it. In New York, Domingo knew, it was always cheaper to kill something than to save it. He popped a menthol cough drop into his mouth and sucked it to nothing. It burned the small sore in his cheek that wouldn't heal.

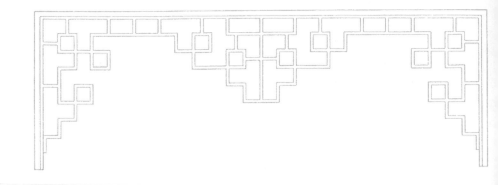

The Lucky Find

HAVANA
(1867–1868)

A negress (with her first child) young and robust, birthed six weeks ago, good and abundant milk, very regular cook, basic principles of sewing, excellent handservant, particular skills, healthy and without vices: Calle San Juan de Dios n. 84.

S hortly after reading the advertisement in *El Diario de la Marina*, Chen Pan closed up his secondhand shop and went to inspect the slave and her child at Calle San Juan de Dios. He'd seen notices for slaves before, next to rewards for run-away servants and ads for horses and plows, but never a mother for sale with her baby.

The blazing sun bored through Chen Pan's new Panama hat. The rainbow of awnings stretching across the street offered only intermittent relief. Chen Pan could have hired a *volante* to take him across town, but he much preferred to walk. A chain gang of slaves trudged over the cobblestones, scattering children and a loose parrot in the dust. Chen Pan touched the knife he kept in his vest pocket and stared at the overseer. His day would come, maybe sooner than the criollos feared.

The vendors hawked fresh okra and star apples, sugarplums, parakeets, and pigs' feet. Lottery tickets were for sale alongside the fruit preserves made by the country *mulatas*. There was a contortionist on a square of carpet, twisted like a *buñuelo*. Another man sold *cocullos,* giant fireflies, six for twenty-five cents. Twine-muzzled donkeys were strung nose to tail, barely visible beneath their burdens of fodder. Everywhere Chen Pan went, the grumous smell of salted beef thickened the air.

A Chinese peddler sauntered by with toasted pea-nuts: *"¡Mani tosta'o caliente, pa' la vieja que no tiene dientes!"* A newcomer with a queue trailed after him with an identical basket. *"¡Lo mismo!"* he shouted. "Same for me!" Other Chinese sold vegetables from baskets hung on bamboo poles. One skin-and-bones in floppy slippers juggled dishes, his pale green pottery clattering as he walked. The ginger vendor nodded when he saw Chen Pan. Others did, too. Everyone knew him in Chinatown.

His regular customers called him *un chino aplatanado*, a Chinese transplant. The recent arrivals from China wanted to be like him, rich and unflinching. From them, Chen Pan heard heart-sorrow stories. Famine and civil war were rampant back home, they reported. Long-haired rebels were destroying everything. Boys were being kidnapped and carried from their plows against their will. There were mutinies on the high seas. Death voyages. Devil ships. On one journey, there was nothing to eat on board except rice. *They thought we ate only rice!*

Six years ago, Chen Pan had left the forest the same day he'd killed the *jutía*. He'd cut off his queue and stopped dreaming of returning to his village. After two years on the plantation and nearly another battling his mother's ghost, what else could be as hard? It had taken him four months more to work his way to the capital—hauling scrap metal, grooming gamecocks, and furiously gambling. Chen Pan never understood what the sight of Havana, with its seductive curve of coast, stirred in him; only that from the moment he arrived, he knew it was where he belonged.

O n Calle Barcelona, Chen Pan stopped to buy a cigar twice the length of his middle finger. It burned slowly and evenly, warming his lungs as he strolled. A handsome woman in a chiffon dress stepped from her carriage on the corner of Calle Villegas with several servants in tow. A *calsero,* wearing a red jacket and shiny black thigh boots, sat in the driver's seat. The woman brandished her silk fan before entering the pharmacy with her entourage.

Thirty-five pesos for the fan, Chen Pan thought, maybe forty in mint condition. Wherever he went, Chen Pan priced everything. Sooner or later, he knew, it would end up in his shop.

At the Lucky Find, he sold all manner of heirlooms and oddities: ancient braziers, powdered wigs from long-dead judges, French porcelains, coats of arms, plaster saints with withering expressions, patri-archal busts (frequently noseless), hand-carved cornices, and a variety of costumes and accoutrements. Occasionally, Chen Pan perused the city's streets for abandoned gems, but the pickings were no longer so plentiful. More often, he checked the newspapers for the funeral announcements of illustrious men, then approached the widows with cash for their treasures to help settle their husbands' debts.

Chen Pan had begun by collecting cast-off furniture and bric-a-brac in the back alleys of Havana.

He'd fixed broken dressers one day, polished rusting urns the next, resoled old riding boots. Then he'd dragged his refurbished wares from door to door in his dilapidated wooden cart. At night he'd slept on Calle Baratillo, near the palace where the Count de Santovenia once hosted a three-day feast that ended with a sunset ride in a gas-filled balloon.

Early one Sunday, Chen Pan had saved the count from a bandit's assault. As a reward, the count had offered him protection for life. In this way Chen Pan had obtained his Letter of Domicile, which guaranteed his freedom. Then with the count's support and the money Chen Pan won playing *botón,* he'd opened his shop.

There'd been only a few businesses on Calle Zanja then, mostly fruit stands and a laundry. Now there were four Chinese restaurants, a shoemaker, a barber, several greengrocers, and a specialty shop where Chen Pan bought dried squid and duck's feet. For steamed dumplings, he went to Paco Pang's place (which everyone called Dogs Won't Touch 'Em). And for his red wine, Chen Pan patronized the Bottomless Cup because they served the best eggs pickled in brine.

Chen Pan noticed a young harpist plucking out a discordant tune behind the *rejas* of her mansion. The windows of all the finest houses in Havana were embellished with wrought-iron grates. On the plantation the criollos had locked up the slaves, but here in the city they locked *themselves* in. Against whom were they protecting themselves? Chen Pan understood them too well. Without a second thought, the criollos took the lives of others to ensure their own survival. Then in defending themselves, bad somehow became good.

In the interior patio of another house, double rows of cane-bottom rockers (ninety pesos for a used one in good condition) were occupied by gossiping women of all ages. A few pulled ivory combs through their hair. Others did needlework or watched the passersby with feigned disinterest. The women looked harmless, but they could be as wicked as their brothers. (How many innocent slaves had been put to death by these dainty ladies' accusations?) At dusk they crowded into their carriages in a cloud of lace and perfume and rode along the Paseo Prado to the Plaza de Armas, redolent of gardenias, to listen to the parading military bands play their polkas and marches.

A *chino* like Chen Pan in a white linen suit and a Panama hat was something of a spectacle, like a talking monkey or a sheep in evening dress. Many people glared at him before turning their heads. The Spaniards were the worst, often pelting the Chinese with stones. Chen Pan, though, was too well dressed for them to menace. (He made a point of dressing well.) And the police, who normally arrested dapper *chinos* on charges of gambling, were under strict orders from the powerful De Santovenias to leave him alone.

Chen Pan knew that the Cubans would have preferred that he still worked for them in the fields, or sold garlic at their kitchen doors. The manner in which they spoke to him—and expected to be spoken to in return—infuriated him. But he had learned to control his temper. A gracious tip of his hat was more unsettling to the enemy than a stream of curses, and impossible to retaliate against.

The criollos managed to find other uses for the Chinese. They relied on the herbalists and acupuncturists of Calle Zanja when their own remedies proved worthless. Everyone knew that *los chinos* had special unguents for sore joints, roots with abortive properties, seeds to rid the intestines of parasites. And their fire-heated needles relieved the worst cases of arthritis.

The house where the slave girl worked was freshly painted in yellow and lavender. Lucky colors, Chen Pan thought. Next door was a convent with crumbling walls where pigeons stirred and shed feathers among the ancient stones. The bell in the convent tower struck twelve as Chen Pan knocked on the door. Soon the siesta would claim all of Havana.

Don Joaquín Alomá seemed surprised to see Chen Pan. He looked him up and down and immediately demanded one thousand pesos for his slave and her baby. No doubt, Chen Pan thought, he was trying to take him for a fool.

"I'd like to see the girl first," he said. "And the child, too."

A moment later, Don Joaquín shoved the girl forward and crudely pointed out her attributes. "You can cancel the milkman with this heifer in your house."

One thousand pesos was too much money, Chen Pan knew, but for once he didn't bargain. He took note of the girl's feet, wide with calluses an inch thick. Nothing like his mother's shriveled lotuses. Her name was Lucrecia. She was long-legged and wide-hipped and had a star-shaped scar on her temple.

"How did you get that?" Chen Pan asked.

"She's prone to accidents," Don Joaquín interrupted. "Don't worry, she hurts no one but herself."

"What's your son's name?" Chen Pan tried to catch the girl's eye, but her head was bowed too low.

Don Joaquín grabbed the boy and thrust him at Chen Pan. "See, he never cries. In a couple of years you could put him to work as well. Then breed his mother with a few young bucks and populate your own plantation!"

Chen Pan ignored him. If he bought the girl and paid her a small salary, would she still be considered a slave? It might be handy to have a woman at his place, to clean and cook his meals. Perhaps he could train her to help him in his shop. Chen Pan was on the verge of firing his Spanish assistant. Federico Véa worked only limited hours and refused to use an abacus, insisting on calculating everything in his head. Moreover, Chen Pan distrusted the way Véa's tongue slipped and stalled on every syllable.

Don Joaquín cleared his throat as he counted Chen Pan's money on the solid mahogany table (worth five hundred pesos, at least). Then he gave him the writ of ownership. "Now get out of here, you dirty *chino!*"

Chen Pan turned and looked at the girl. *"Vámonos,"* he said.

Lucrecia bundled her son in a scrap of flannel and followed Chen Pan out the door. The air was as dense as old paint. Lucrecia turned to face the convent, where a nun, snow-white as an egret, nodded to her from a balcony. Chen Pan noticed a mole the size of a peppercorn on the back of Lucrecia's neck, just below her blue cotton turban. Beyond her, thin clouds curled in the sky.

"¿Como se llama?" Chen Pan asked her again, bringing his face close to the boy's. His eyes were brown and alert, two coffee beans.

"Víctor Manuel," she whispered.

Sweet rabbit! Maybe, Chen Pan thought, he could

pretend to be his father. He pointed out a pair of crows to the boy in a breadfruit tree, but Lucrecia shielded his eyes, then crossed herself twice. Chen Pan wondered what sort of foolishness the nuns had taught her. In Chinatown, the Protestant missionaries besieged him constantly with the decrees of their god, Jesus Christ. But Chen Pan distrusted all forms of certainty.

Lucrecia trailed him through the streets, staying three or four steps behind him. The stores were closing their doors to the midday heat. Peddlers jostled for Chen Pan's attention. Tangerines. Dried snake meat. Fresh eggs from the outskirts of town. One by one, they set down their loads to stare at him and Lucrecia walking by.

"To hell with all of you!" Chen Pan sputtered, and returned their stink-eyes.

Chen Pan's home was not fancy, inside or out. He lived in three rooms over the Lucky Find. In this way he saved money, afforded more merchandise, issued loans to other *chinos* for a nominal fee. Chen Pan believed that if you spread a bit of money around, blessings grew. To hoard it was to invite disaster. His furnishings were sparse—a hardwood table and chair, an iron bedstead with a plank bottom, a wash basin, and a worn velvet divan he'd salvaged from Calle Manrique. In the kitchen, he'd set up a modest altar for the Buddha.

He also kept a pet she-duck named Lady Ban. She protected the wood beams by eating the termites and guarded Chen Pan's shop at night. "The slightest rattle and Lady Ban is up in arms," he told everyone. "She's a regular Manchu warrior!"

"Don't eat the duck," Chen Pan instructed Lucrecia on their first day together. He pointed at Lady Ban. "This duck is not for eating." But he wasn't sure that she understood what he said. The girl had barely uttered a word since he'd purchased her on Calle San Juan de Dios.

"*¿No entiende?*" Chen Pan asked impatiently. She returned his question with a stare. What language would he need to speak with her? Chen Pan showed Lucrecia the shallow pan of sand where Lady Ban relieved herself. It would need to be cleaned out, he explained, every other day.

Chen Pan thought of how a man could start out with one idea—like sailing off to Cuba to get rich enough to return home an important man—and end up with another life altogether. This never could have happened in China. There the future was always a loyal continuation of the past.

Lucrecia rocked the baby as Chen Pan showed her their quarters. "Rest," he said, indicating the sagging bed near the window. "This is where you and your son will stay." She sat down on the edge of the bed, her milk-swollen breasts rubbing against her muslin shift. The baby yawned so wide his tiny mouth trembled.

Chen Pan went downstairs to the Lucky Find. In his absence, the Spanish assistant had reopened the shop and sold a musty oil painting and a seventeenth-century map to a tourist from Boston. One hundred sixty pesos for both. Chen Pan was pleased, although he suspected Véa of pocketing a portion of the sale.

He took the money and went to the market, to a stall that sold toys and children's clothes. Chen Pan selected a wooden train, a rag-stuffed horse with a painted grin, calf-leather shoes, and a minuscule linen suit. He ordered all of it delivered to his shop in an hour.

Then he visited a fabric kiosk. *Basic principles of sewing.* Chen Pan tried to remember all the fripperies he removed from the whores on Calle Rayos. Voluminous dresses with endless ribbons and bows. Satin corsets with whalebone stays. Lace petticoats. Bustles that made their *nalgas* swell. Beneath all this were slips and silk stockings rolled above the knee. So many buttons and fasteners to undo, it frustrated the clumsier men.

Lucky for Chen Pan, his fingers were nimble. The ladies favored him. Plump dumpling girls were what

71

he liked now. He hated to feel any ribs whatsoever. He went for the older ones, twenty-five and up. No paying two hundred pesos for a virgin like some of his friends. A waste of money, in his opinion. The ladies praised Chen Pan for not ripping their garments. No violent pushing, either. Smooth tiger from China. Never left a bruise.

Chen Pan bought forty yards of gingham, another twenty of a fine scarlet satin. Assorted fluff and ribbons for the underthings. A brand-new pair of scissors. A tin box filled with needles, buttons, and thread.

On his way home, he stopped at a restaurant called Bendición for meat pies, tamales, and sweet potato fritters. Chen Pan was perplexed by the names Cubans gave their shops. La Rectitud. La Buena Fé. Todos Me Elogian. How could anybody guess what was sold inside? Once he'd walked into a shop called La Mano Poderosa, only to find huge wheels of Portuguese cheese for sale.

Lucrecia had swept the apartment clean and was chopping an onion in the kitchen when Chen Pan returned. *Very regular cook.* He watched as she peeled and diced two potatoes, dropped them into a pot for soup. In a few days, he would teach her how to make milk pudding for his breakfast. And in the spring, when fresh bamboo shoots were available in Havana, he'd show her how to cook them in a great earthen pot with boiling rice.

A whimpering came from the bedroom. Lucrecia went to her son and settled him at her breast. He suckled eagerly, his fists resting possessively on her chest. Chen Pan showed Lucrecia his purchases, offered her a stretch of the satin to touch. She didn't admire the fabric. Instead she stared at him again, her lips pressed together by the icy muscles of her face.

There was a loud knocking downstairs. It was Federico Véa. The Lucky Find was crowded with tourists from England who needed Chen Pan's assistance. What the British considered precious amused Chen Pan: silver letter openers with strangers' initials and farm animal figurines. They would pay a premium, it seemed, for anything sporting a pig. He noticed that their teeth were small and mossy, like woodland creatures'.

After they left, Véa complained that nothing at the Lucky Find had a fixed price. How could he be expected to remember figures that changed from one hour to the next?

"Those pigs you sold for fifty pesos apiece were ten pesos yesterday," he huffed.

"Of course they went up!" Chen Pan bellowed back. "The price is what a customer needs to pay!"

When he returned to his apartment, Víctor Manuel was asleep. Chen Pan arranged the baby's clothes and the rag horse for him at the foot of the bed. Lucrecia watched him closely.

"¿Que quiere con nosotros?" Her voice could have sharpened knives.

"Nada. I want nothing." Chen Pan wasn't sure this was true, but could he simply set them free?

Lucrecia ate her food in silence, gave him no thanks, stiffly rinsed the dishes. Then she slept, fully dressed, curled around her infant son, her coarse hair spread loose on the pillow. Chen Pan forswore his usual cups of red wine and settled on the velvet divan. For once, he insisted that Lady Ban sleep by herself in the kitchen.

He thought of going to Madame Yvette's. It was Thursday night and the voluptuous Delmira from Güines would be there. Maybe he should take *her* the river of satin. She'd know how to thank him. Chen Pan thought of Delmira's rained-on earth scent, her kindling thighs. Best of all, Chen Pan loved the salve of her pink padded lips working every inch of his *pinga* before swallowing him whole.

A bright half-moon shone through the window. The wind raved, tearing the leaves off the palms, altering the sky. Chen Pan recalled how years ago, a fierce windstorm had coated his family's wheat fields with dust. The same day, his father had claimed that he'd procured a magical herb that would enable him to remember everything he'd ever read. Before he could test its efficacy, the bandits had come. By nightfall they'd severed Father's head with a sword, parading it on a pole for the entire village to see.

When you remembered a wind, Chen Pan thought bitterly, it blew forever.

Had Chen Pan gone mad? Soon that was the word in Chinatown. Over the next few weeks his fellow merchants visited him, trying to dissuade him from his imprudence. Chen Pan listened to them, treated them to warmed wine at the Bottomless Cup in return for their admonitions. But he didn't change his mind.

"Too much heat is simmering in your head!" the grocer Pedro Pla Tan warned him. He advised Chen Pan to get a proper wife from China or, better yet, to visit the new whorehouse on Calle Teniente Rey. Why invite trouble by buying this slave? There was a French girl just arrived at Madame Yvette's, a fourteen-year-old natural blonde who wore red lace panties slit in two. "Her waist is like a roll of new silk," Pedro Pla Tan sighed.

The fish seller, Benito Sook, quoted Confucius, who said that it wasn't until a man reached sixty that his ears obeyed him. It was clear, Sook insisted, that Chen Pan's ears were nowhere near obedience.

Sook and the other merchants agreed that Chen

Pan's sentimentality surely would cause a deformity. After all, look at how Evelio Bai's head had so swollen from his love of flattery that he could barely hold it upright. Or how that Ramón Gu's arms had stretched to preternatural lengths from his greediness. And what of the sad example of Felipe Yam, who continued to grow lumps on his breasts from sheer indolence?

Yes, the men agreed, Chen Pan would suffer this decision. At the very least he would be plagued with backaches and blurred vision, a sore neck, a dizzy head, a parched tongue.

On her first morning at the Lucky Find, Lucrecia knocked over a marble bust of a Spanish general, prompting the patriotic Véa to quit on the spot. Lucrecia swept up the broken pieces, then continued dusting from one tenebrous end of the store to the other. But each time she turned around, Lucrecia knocked another heirloom to the ground. Only a bronze Moroccan elephant, defenselessly sprawled on its back, escaped with just a minor dent.

How could she be so good with a knife, Chen Pan wondered, and ox-clumsy in his shop?

"The air is nervous in here," Lucrecia said, unsettling the stale air of centuries with her feather duster. She insisted that the objects in Chen Pan's store confessed their miseries to her. The Virgin of Regla statue loathed the drunkard sculptor who'd carved her face into a grimace. And the mantilla draped over that gilded mirror had once belonged to a flamenco dancer who'd lost her left leg to gangrene.

"Foolish girl!" Chen Pan interrupted her. "Talking to knickknacks!" For days she'd said nothing at all, and now this?

When Lucrecia went upstairs to prepare his lunch, Chen Pan brought his ear to the Virgin's lips. For him, though, there was nothing but a stagnant silence.

A week later, with his inventory in near shambles and the baby's squalling fraying his nerves (Chen Pan, too, had begun breaking his share of antiquities), he asked Lucrecia, "What else can you do?"

"I make candles," she said. It was a skill she'd learned with the Sisters of Affliction.

Chen Pan bought everything she needed to get started. There was slow-burning string, beeswax, assorted dyes, a copper cauldron, flexible scrapers, and a wooden drying rack. Then he set up a workshop for her in the back of the Lucky Find.

Before long, Lucrecia was peddling her candles all over Havana. For Easter, she made pastel tapers dipped in vanilla and rose oil. By June, she was selling votives scented with crushed orange blossoms and calling them *velas de amor.* Word spread among the city's savviest women of the candles' stimulating effects in the boudoir. Every Thursday when Lucrecia offered a fresh batch of her love candles for sale, women came from everywhere to secure their week's supply.

In July, Lucrecia announced to Chen Pan that she'd gone to the magistrate to have herself evaluated. Chen Pan knew what that meant. *Una coartación.* Lucrecia wanted to buy her and Víctor Manuel's freedom.

"You're free to go today," he told her. "I won't hold you here against your will." Lucrecia didn't answer him, but she also didn't leave.

Instead Lucrecia planted a garden behind the Lucky Find. Yuca. Taro root. Black-eyed peas. Three types of beans. No ornamental flowers whatsoever. She said she would grow only what they could eat.

Chen Pan insisted that she plant chrysanthemums like his great-aunt had in China. The flowers bloomed in the fall and promoted longevity, he told her. His great-aunt had drunk wine infusions made from the sweet-smelling petals and had lived well into her eighties.

Lucrecia reluctantly planted a bed of chrysanthemums to honor Chen Pan's wishes, but the flowers quickly wilted in the summer heat.

Víctor Manuel grew to be a strong boy. He began walking at nine months. One step, two steps, then down in a heap. He never bothered to crawl. His legs were fat with rolls. Sturdy as two dynasties, Chen Pan laughed. It pleased him to squeeze them. Víctor Manuel liked the sound of the drums, of the lute and the Chinese *sheng* pipes, and so Chen Pan paid musicians to come and play for the boy in the mornings.

"Sa! Sa!" Víctor Manuel imitated the lute player, sounding like the wind blowing through the rain. *"Ch'ieh! Ch'ieh!"* he shouted when the notes climbed as high as the voices of chattering ghosts. The boy swayed and rocked with the swelling notes and cried when the lute player went home.

On Saturdays, Chen Pan took Víctor Manuel with him to Arturo Fu Fon's barbershop for a trim and a fresh round of gossip. Víctor Manuel followed the talk, eyeing each man in turn as though assessing the worthiness of his information. Chen Pan was convinced that the boy would be speaking perfect Chinese soon.

"Perfect Chinese with this bunch of woolly heads?" Arturo Fu Fon laughed, folding his hands over his generous stomach. "Poor little cricket. Who'll talk to him after we're gone?"

At the barbershop, the men were most fond of discussing naval disasters. They speculated on the fate of the *Flora Temple,* shipwrecked with eight hundred fifty Chinese aboard. Or the *Hong Kong,* which ran aground after the recruits set it on fire. Most mysterious was the case of *El Fresneda.* Shortly after leaving Macao, the frigate disappeared. Months later, the British navy found it drifting off the coast of the Philippines with one hundred fifty skeletons on board.

"People will devour each other when there's nothing else to eat," Arturo Fu Fon said, sliding his razor down the cheek of the remarkably hirsute Tomás Lai.

"Wouldn't there be somebody left after picking all those bones clean?" asked Eduardo Tsen. He came to the barbershop only to argue.

"A man today, tomorrow a cockroach or a hungry ghost," Salustiano Chung predicted from beneath his gauze hat. Then he turned to Chen Pan with a grin. "And what do you think, Señor Chen?"

Everyone laughed. Their routine was already well worn.

"As the great philosopher Lao-tzu once said," Chen Pan began, " 'Those who speak know nothing. Those who know are silent.' "

"Yes, and those who speak of the virtues of silence are themselves cockatoos!" Arturo Fu Fon chimed in.

When they forgot their shipwrecks, the men spoke longingly of home. The lowliest *chino* in Cuba knew by heart Li Po's poem:

> *Before my bed*
> *there is bright moonlight*
> *So that it seems*
> *like frost on the ground:*

Lifting my head
I watch the bright moon,
Lowering my head
I dream that I'm home.

Most of Chen Pan's friends had been farmers in China, and no amount of city excitement could replace for them the quiet pleasures of working the soil. Chen Pan, however, wasn't the least bit nostalgic. He was most grateful to Cuba for this: to be freed, at last, from the harsh cycles of the land. He'd carried both books and a hoe in his youth. He preferred the books.

When he was a boy, the elders in his village had tried to foretell the harvest by interpreting the movement of beans they tossed in the air, or by puff-roasting rice in an iron pan. They listened to the timbre of thunder linking the old year with the new, then made their prognostications. But there was no predicting the inconstant proportions of sun and rain, the continual affliction of floods. And their palm-bark coats did little to protect them from the weather. In bad times, children were sold to pay the rent, and everyone chewed boiled wheat to calm their empty stomachs.

Chen Pan no longer believed in demons that ruined the harvest, that food eaten from one's own toil tasted best. He would rather buy a single yam and roast it plain for his dinner than resign himself to the unpredictability of the land. He preferred to pay his weekly bribe to the Cuban policeman, too (a rather modest sum on account of the De Santovenias), than surrender his entire farm to the Emperor's tax collectors.

Víctor Manuel's birthday coincided with the Chinese New Year. What could be luckier? Plump, brown, healthy boy. Firecrackers popping all around. Pyramids of oranges and pomegranates. A red satin birthday suit sewn for him with silk thread and tassels. A miniature jade baton to ensure a scholarly future.

Chen Pan threw a banquet in the boy's honor, inviting all the esteemed men from Chinatown. They arrived in a slow procession, like self-important elephants. Benny Lan and Lisardo Hu, who owned the biggest restaurant on Calle Zanja. Marcos Jui, the most successful greengrocer. And, of course, the barber Arturo Fu Fon. Chen Pan welcomed his many brothers from the merchants' association: Juan Yip Men, Lázaro Seng, Feliciano Wu, Andrés Tang, Jacinto Kwok. Even the Count de Santovenia stopped by with a gift.

In the glow of the colored lanterns, every kind of special dish was served. Fried baby pigeons. Chopped lobster. Jellyfish with cucumber. Shark's fin soup. Red bean pudding. Lichees all the way from China. Chen

Pan gave his guests boiled gold water to drink so that they would continue to prosper, offered them blessings to last a thousand years. Arturo Fu Fon proposed a toast: "May death be long in coming but abrupt when it finally arrives!"

The men ate and drank, belched and laughed until their eyes watered—at their hardships, at their good fortune, at the many grandsons they hoped would surround them in old age. No man there, though, had the heart or the bitter nerve to remind Chen Pan that Víctor Manuel was not really his son. That, in fact, he had no children at all.

After dinner, the men settled in to tell their stories. Lázaro Seng spoke of an uncle who had cured his mother's dysentery by making soup using flesh cut from his own thigh. Jacinto Kwok recalled how in his village a neighbor had been flayed alive for slapping his mother, another exiled at the mere request of his father. Only in China, the men agreed, was life lived properly.

Listening to his friends, Chen Pan questioned whether he was genuinely Chinese anymore. It was true that he'd left his sorry patch of wheat half a world away, but in ten years he'd built a new life entirely from muscle and cunning. This much Chen Pan knew: a man's fate could change overnight; only the mountains stayed the same forever.

The following autumn, a deadly plague infested Havana. Half the street vendors in Chinatown died within a week. People blamed the river that coursed through the city, corpses and filth floating in it. The wealthy fled to their country homes, avoided all contact with the poor. But the sickness did not discriminate between rich and poor.

One morning, a rash like a fine brocade erupted on Víctor Manuel's back, and his belly swelled melonhard. Chen Pan ran to find the doctor from S——. By the time they returned, the boy was shaking and his short pants were soaked with blood. The doctor boiled a pot of odoriferous roots and held Víctor Manuel over the steam. He prescribed fresh lemon juice and cane syrup for him to drink.

"I'll protect you like a ghost," Chen Pan swore to the boy in Chinese. He strung up a tightly woven fisherman's net over Víctor Manuel's bed so that as he slept, his spirit couldn't leave his body. But despite Chen Pan's vigilance, the boy's spirit seemed to be escaping in wisps.

At midnight, Chen Pan put his ear to Víctor Manuel's mouth. Not a whisper of breath. He clutched him to his chest, forced his own air into the boy's lungs. How could this be? Chen Pan prayed to the Buddha, beseeched him for one more hour with his son. When nature is not respected, Chen Pan cried, the heart grows empty, night outlasts daylight.

> *There's no swordstroke clarity when grief tears*
>   *the heart,*
> *and tears darkening my eyes aren't rinsing red*
>   *dust away,*
> *but I'm still nurturing emptiness—emptiness of*
>   *heaven's*
> *black black, this childless life stretching away*
>   *before me.*

The next day the Protestant missionaries came around, wielding their Bibles and explanations. Chen Pan shouted for them to leave.

"Their god must be lonely in heaven," Lucrecia said after the missionaries fled. "Who could love such a master?" She stayed by Chen Pan's side for many days, neither crying nor praying, simply still.

A t the barbershop, Chen Pan's friends didn't know how to console him. Their talk turned instead to the war that had broken out against Spain. Carlos Manuel de Céspedes, a respected landowner, had freed his slaves so they could join the struggle. Others were following suit. Chen

Pan recalled the forced conscriptions in China, the young men sent far to the north, to lands of interminable winters and roaring bears.

His friends applauded the feats of Captain Liborio Wong, the Chinese botanical doctor who'd helped recapture Bayamo during the early weeks of the war. Of the bravery of Commander Sebastián Sian, who they'd heard had killed three Spaniards—*pa! pa! pa!*—with the back of his sword. They imagined themselves riding into battle on stallions bridled in gold. Of fashioning drinking cups from enemy skulls, as their ancestors had done against Yüeh-chih, the defeated king of Han times. Of perfecting their shooting until the very birds would be afraid to fly.

But not a single one joined the fighting.

"The great thing isn't fame or fortune but stamina," Arturo Fu Fon said. "In Cuba, it's enough just to survive."

For ten days Chen Pan hardly ate or slept. He thought of leaving the island altogether. Of what use was he if he couldn't save a helpless child? Chen Pan had heard of other *chinos* sailing ships around Indonesia, working the mines in South Africa, building the railroads that crisscrossed North America. Hard work that would leave no time for mourning.

At least in Cuba, it was warm everywhere, and he knew it was impossible to starve. Chen Pan reached down and felt the muscles in his legs. He'd gotten much too soft in Havana, fussing endlessly with delicate things in his shop. Could he regain his forest strength? The necessary sinew for battle?

On the eleventh day, Chen Pan put Lucrecia in charge of the Lucky Find. He strode over to Calle Muralla, purchased fifty machetes, and hired a two-horse cart and driver. Then, against Lucrecia's objections, Chen Pan headed east, toward the war, to deliver the machetes to Commander Sian.

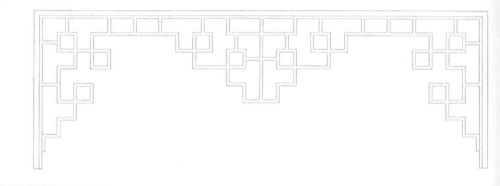

Middle Kingdom

Chen Fang

SHANGHAI
(1924)

In the mountain village where I grew up, my mother smoked opium. She'd grown accustomed to the money my father, Lorenzo Chen, used to send her from Cuba. My two older sisters married early and left for their husbands' homes. They are traditional women, obedient to their men and eldest sons. They have bound feet and never traveled far.

I am not like my sisters. When I was born, the midwife, soaked to her elbows in birthing blood, called out: "Another mouth for rice!" My mother was so distraught that she dropped me on my head. My brow swelled and I took a fever, but still I lived. The same evening, my grandmother died. Mother thought me an evil presence and refused to nurse me. Instead I was given oxen milk to drink. For this reason I grew so obstinate.

My oldest sister was just three when our father left China for good. First Sister said she remembered how his hair smelled of oranges. Father had returned from his travels for the Full Month celebration after my birth, and a pyramid of oranges stood tall in my honor. Mother had dressed me in red-and-gold silk and hosted a feast that lasted three days. She'd told Father that I was a boy.

Every villager went along with the deceit. A third daughter in as many years certainly meant bad luck. But no one wanted my father retracting his promise to build a new well for the village. I, of course, remember nothing of him. Father returned to Cuba when I was four months old. By then he had taken a second wife, a soup seller he'd met in the streets of Canton. Together they left China on a merchant ship.

I had a great deal of freedom as a child. Mother dressed me as a boy, treated me as a boy, and soon everyone seemed to forget that I was a girl. She did not bind my feet, and I was allowed to play with the rough boys who caught wild bees in the fields. I did not help in the kitchen. I did not learn how to sew. And only I, of my sisters, went to school. My father sent extra money for this purpose, to educate his oldest son.

"I don't want him plowing the fields like a peasant," he wrote. And so it was.

At school, I was praised for my calligraphy. I understood intuitively the sway and press of the brush, the precise images they conjured up. One of the first characters I learned was "home." It looked to me like a pig with a roof over its head. It is meant to spell contentment.

My father was very methodical about sending Mother money. During the leanest years, we had rice and steamed buns and a little meat to eat. His letters arrived twice a year. The envelopes were trimmed with fancy stamps of rubied hummingbirds and skeletal palms and thickly bearded men. My sisters and I showed off the stamps to the other children in the village.

Once he sent us a photograph of our grandfather, Chen Pan. I had heard many stories about him. That

he had been kidnapped in China and enslaved on a
large farm in Cuba. That he had escaped the farm
after killing three white men. That he had survived
for years as a fugitive in the woods, eating nothing
but hairless creatures that swung through the trees.
That he became rich after saving a Spanish lady's
honor, although he never succeeded in marrying her.
That he was, miraculously, still alive.

"Will I ever get to meet him?" I asked my mother.

But she wouldn't answer me, losing herself instead
to the sweet blue smoke.

From an early age I dreamed of running away, of
joining my father in Cuba. Mother said that I looked
like him, especially when I was unhappy. My lips
would purse together, pinching my face in a most disagreeable manner. She showed me the picture of their
wedding day. The two of them are posed formally on a
lacquered bench with pots of chrysanthemums on
either side. Father is tall and thin, and his skin is a
faded brown.

The villagers gossiped about his mother, who had
been a slave in Cuba before ensnaring a full-blooded
Chinese. They said that all the slaves there worked
the sugarcane fields harder than any beast, that
they boiled human flesh on feast days, then gathered
around their simmering kettles and banged on a hundred drums.

There were other tales about Cuba. How fish that

rained from the sky during thunderstorms had to be shoveled off the roads before they rotted. How seeds dropped in the ground one day would shoot up green the next. How gold was so plentiful that the Cubans used it for buttons and broom handles. And when a woman fancied a man, she signaled to him with her fan. In Havana, the women chose whom they would marry and when.

Everything I heard about Cuba made my head revolve with dreams. How badly I wanted to go!

By the time I was nine, the teacher in our village informed my mother that he had taught me all he knew. He implored her to send me to a boys' academy several days away by cart and train. It was a school in the old tradition, once renowned for preparing scholars for the Imperial examinations.

Mother wrote to my father, requesting a decision. That summer he pledged money for ten more years of schooling. I am quite certain that he would not have promised this if he had known I was a girl. The fact remains that I owe everything I am to his generosity.

I was the best student at my boarding school. I excelled in mathematics and Confucian philosophy and studied English and French. It was not easy to disguise my sex. I kept my hair cropped short and affected a gruff manner, but my hands and neck were too delicate for a boy. My size helped. I was a head taller than most of the other students and I was not afraid to fight.

In the spring of my fifteenth year, our literature teacher, Professor Hou, took twelve of us to Canton to see the opera and visit historical sites. One morning, word spread that a fellow student had discovered a brothel that catered to virgins. Well, every last scholar dropped his books and followed him out of the lodgment!

The brothel was in a plain wooden house, not far from the marketplace. Long scrolls of painted silk decorated the walls, including one of an idyllic mountain gorge. A faint breeze made the silk flutter in place.

One by one, my classmates were escorted into the same squalid room. It was big enough for a bedroll and a tray of steaming tea. No one remained inside longer than a few minutes. Each boy pretended to be more pleased than confused when he came out.

When it was my turn, I was astonished to see the bare, slender back of a girl no older than me. Her hair was coiled and messily fastened with jade pins. She turned toward me. Her eyes were smeared black, her lips smudged the color of sunset. Even in the distorting shadows of the room, I found her beautiful. *Lovely as a blossom born of clouds.*

She opened her mouth and gestured with her tongue. I approached her slowly. She took my hand and rubbed it against her breasts. I felt a jolt go through me. Then she touched me between my thighs.

"Who are you?" she asked me sharply, pulling her hand away.

"A girl," I told her. "Please tell no one."

We were silent a long time.

"Why are you here?"

"Everyone thinks I'm a boy. It's the only way I can study."

To my surprise, the girl patted the bedroll beside her.

"Stay a while," she said. "This way the others will think you're a man." She began to giggle.

I stared at her mouth, her small, uneven teeth. She stared back at me and grew quiet again. Her breathing was slow and steady. Mine was rapid, erratic.

"Do you like being a boy?" she asked.

"It's all I know," I answered.

She took my hand again, holding it tightly as we waited together in silence. The air smelled faintly sweet.

Finally, there was a knock at the door. I stood up, bowed deeply, and left.

That autumn, my mother sent me a letter. "Come home," it said. "There is no more money to study." There was a war in the West, and my father's remittances had ceased. It was time, she said, that I married.

Mother had betrothed me to a young man who lived two days' journey north of our village. To explain my absence, she had told his family that I was away helping a sick relative in the city. They would pay a fine dowry, my mother wrote, enough to take care of her in her dotage. But I knew where my dowry money would go: in a cloud of opium smoke.

I stared at the black ink against the coarse parchment. Again I thought of escaping to Cuba, but I had no money and my father knew only that I was an intelligent boy. The letter was in the handwriting of the local scribe. Through him, the village knew everyone's affairs. The scribe lived in a hut by a stream high on a mountain ledge. Everyone said that water demons resided there.

Outside my dormitory window was an ancient oak, the leaves stained red with the advancing season. The winter before, a sixth-year boy had hanged himself from the tree after failing his final examinations. I remembered how peaceful he had looked swaying in the wind. I imagined climbing onto the same branch, rope in hand, summoning dead spirits to strengthen me. Then the sudden pressure around my neck, a last gasp of breath, the blackening release.

1 was sixteen when I went home and married Lu Shêng-pao. His family had a big house with pine trees that sang on windy days. It was not easy to become a woman. I was not trained to pour tea or be graceful in the usual deferences. I could not cook, and my sewing was crooked. My hair was wavy and hard to control.

Worst of all were my unbound feet. For this, my mother-in-law ridiculed me: "We wouldn't have paid so much for you if we'd seen those clumsy hooves!"

This I must say directly. There is no harder work than being a woman. I know this because I pretended to be a boy for so long. This is what men do: pretend to be men, hide their weaknesses at all costs. A man would sooner kill or die himself than suffer embarrassment. For women there are no such blusterings, only work.

How sad it is to be a woman!
Nothing on earth is held so cheap.
Boys stand leaning at the door
Like Gods fallen out of Heaven.

Lu Shêng-pao was the third of four sons. He worked in his father's textiles shop, but he had no passion for this. Behind the rice paper screen of our room, he liked to read and draw. I was lucky. Lu Shêng-pao demanded very little of me. Our first night together, he planted his seed in me once and never tried again.

My mother-in-law kept a meticulous calendar and soon announced at dinner that my monthly blood had stopped. I looked out the window. The garden was bright with peonies, their stems bending with heavy blossoms. I thought of how flowers in full bloom were most ready to die. The sun was setting. The horizon, it seemed to me, neatly divided the living from the dead.

News of the pregnancy improved my worth in the eyes of my husband's family. A daughter-in-law so fertile brings good fortune, signifies that the gods have approved the match. Before me, the family's luck had not been good. First Brother's wife had died of the coughing sickness. And Second Brother's wife received endless scorn after seven childless winters.

During the first months of my pregnancy, I was so ill and despairing that I ate only a bit of dry rice. Each day seemed heavy and gray, as if the sky had lowered its eaves.

One afternoon Lu Shêng-pao brought home a packet of herbs that he said would settle my stomach.

He boiled the tea himself, something he had never done, and offered it to me in a fine porcelain cup. Then he tucked a blanket around my knees. The tea was hot and fragrant, like a field of wildflowers. It seemed to flow to every corner of my body, warming it, until I grew drowsy and fell into a deep sleep.

That night I woke up with a searing pain down my middle. I groaned and curled forward, felt a stickiness along my thighs. Where was my husband? With trembling hands, I lit the lamp and saw that our bed was wet with blood. I screamed, alerting the whole house.

My mother-in-law stormed in and eased me to the floor mat. "Don't move!" she instructed and disappeared into the darkness. I do not know how long it took her to return with the sleepy herbalist.

Liang Tai-lung wedged a damp poultice between my legs and tied it to my waist with a sash. Then he sprinkled a bitter powder on the back of my tongue. When he lifted the remains of my husband's tea to his nose, he called my mother-in-law aside. She marched over and slapped my face hard.

"How dare you try to kill my grandson!" she screeched. She refused to hear my explanation.

I lay on the floor mat for a month, unable to move. My mother-in-law sent in the maid to change my poultice and empty my chamber pot, which she carefully inspected. She brought my meals herself, making sure I swallowed everything—hearty broths made from chicken livers and bamboo shoots. She was determined that I should live long enough to deliver her first grandchild.

I asked her where Lu Shêng-pao was, but she wouldn't answer me. Later, I learned that he'd been sent to the South on business for his father.

When my belly grew so large I felt as though I had swallowed the moon, Second Sister came to visit me. She had traveled far, suffering on her lotus feet. My mother-in-law was suspicious of her visit, but she permitted us to sit together on the porch. She herself sat nearby, embroidering a silk pillowcase for the baby.

It was a blustery day, and the pines sang like the opera heroine I had heard in Canton. The birds scattered in all directions. The wind kept unsettling my mother-in-law's sewing. When she entered the house to fetch more thread, my sister slipped me a letter from my old professor. Then she kissed me on the cheek and departed. I never saw her again.

I waited until everyone was asleep to retrieve the letter from my sash. Professor Hou had recommended me for a teaching post at a foreigners' school in Shanghai. I was to report there at the start of the New Year, four months hence. I could not still my breathing. I must leave here, I thought. But how?

For the next week, every hour seemed a day and each day a year. I grew clumsier than usual in the kitchen, dropped a platter of steamed asparagus on my feet. My mother-in-law grew concerned. She took me to a fortune-teller, blind and decrepit, who specialized in predicting the sex of the unborn with a cracked tortoiseshell.

"To you a son will be born," she foretold. "He will rule over many people with the sun on his shoulder. But you must leave him after one month. This is the will of your ancestors."

Soon after Lu Chih-mo was born, my mother-in-law paid me handsomely to abandon their home. I left without apologies and took a train to Shanghai. My breasts were painfully hard, leaking with unsupped milk. How often I have suffered this decision! I tried to banish thoughts of my son, of his baby fist around my finger, of his involuntary smiles when he slept. His face was so pale, a mysterious little moon. I thought I would be pleased to leave him, to seek my freedom. Instead I swallowed my bitter heart again and again.

I almost returned to Lu Chih-mo on several occasions. I bought tickets on trains I never boarded, imagined flying over this scarred, warring land to find him playing with a length of knotted string beneath the pines. I thought of stealing him, of bringing him back with me to Shanghai. But I realized that it would be easier for me to see heaven than to see my boy again.

In Shanghai, I was fortunate. I did not hide my gender and still the foreigners hired me, thanks to Professor Hou's kind words.

I teach Chinese classics and modern literatures. My students are the children of diplomats and industrialists: French children, English children, children of wealthy Chinese families, too. I pretend to be a widow. I pretend to be childless. And so people do not concern themselves with my life.

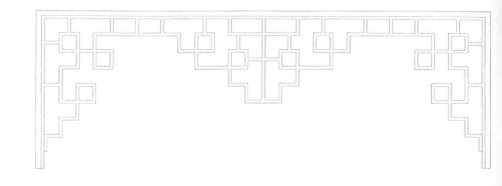

Monkeys

CENTRAL HIGHLANDS, VIETNAM (1969)

Rabo mono amarra mono.

Domingo Chen was on night watch. He volunteered for it often, preferring darkness to the day's uneasy camaraderies. He sat behind his mound of packed red clay, his M-16 oiled and loose in his hands, his flak jacket scrawled with BINGO. A sickle moon played hide-and-seek through the jungle canopy. There were no stars. No way to read heaven with any accuracy. He might have loved this sky in another time, from another perspective.

Domingo listened to the rumble of nightmares from the foxholes, men crying out in their sleep, fear pulling wires in their throats. Lately, there'd been drowsy talk about how the snub-nosed monkeys started howling when the weather shifted, how the peasants hunted the monkeys and sold their skulls as war souvenirs. In Cuba, Domingo recalled, the *paleros* had coveted the skulls of Chinese suicides for their curses and spells.

The day had been hell. During the hot, lacquering afternoon, Danny Spadoto had been blown apart by a booby trap, as though no more than a vague idea had been holding him together. Spadoto had been a superb whistler, a genius with puckered lips. After several beers he would take requests, could do Sinatra's "September Song" note by perfect note. He'd been a big guy with beefy, fluorescent cheeks; a happy guy, even in war. Domingo wondered whether Spadoto had been happy because he'd known a lot more than everyone else, or a lot less.

At lunch they'd switched C rations (his pork slices for Domingo's lamb loaf), and Spadoto had offered Domingo the address of the guaranteed best lay in Saigon. *Hair smells like goddam coconuts,* he'd promised, letting out an awed whistle. Domingo had stared at the scribbled information: Tham Thanh Lan, 14 Nguyen Doc Street. Two hours later, he was shaking Spadoto's torso loose from a breadfruit tree. Domingo had understood then that he would spend the rest of his life trying to walk normally again, trying to lose his slow-motion, anti–land mine strut.

In the afternoon, cutting through a vine-choked path, the rain coming down rice-sticky, the platoon had stumbled onto a field of white flowers. Domingo had sniffed the air. It smelled sea-brackish, although they were nowhere near the ocean. The Vietnamese scout, a square-faced man everyone called Flounder, said that the flowers bloomed once every thirty years. To see them, and in such profusion, meant excellent luck. To everyone's surprise Flounder began eating the flowers, which were salty and curiously thirst-quenching. Salt of the jungle. *Sal de la selva,* Domingo translated to himself, and put one in his mouth. Then a quiet euphoria settled over him until dusk.

Domingo absently rubbed the magazine of his M-16 as he stared into the haze of the jungle. The slow stain of night seeped into his skin. He thought of how his hands hadn't been his in nearly a year, how they hadn't touched a conga or loved a woman in all that time. How mostly they'd just scratched insects from his skin.

Soon it would be the first anniversary of Papi's death. Domingo had visited his grave in the Bronx before leaving for Vietnam. He'd sprinkled the plot with fresh water, burned incense and a handful of new dollar bills, left a crate of fresh papayas he'd bought at a Puerto Rican bodega. He'd given away everything of theirs except for a pair of spectacles that had belonged to his great-grandfather, Chen Pan. Domingo promised himself that he would return in a year to complete the traditional rituals. But only fear, he knew, made promises.

Domingo tried to conjure up images of his father. Papi on the banks of the Río Guaso, guiding Domingo's fishing pole. "Hold the pole steady, *mi hijo.* Wait until the fish rises to the bait." His father's fingers folding the edge of a dumpling or deveining a mound of shrimp. Those same fingers massaging Domingo's scalp "to make your brain work better." Papi's blue (always blue) guayaberas swinging loosely on his skinny frame. The high sheen of the American shoes he'd bought at the naval base. The babyish way he'd suckled his cigarettes.

Then came the images Domingo found unbearable to consider. Papi trembling at the edge of the subway platform, wearing his white linen suit. The approach of the man in the red shirt (that's what the police report said—all details but no explanations) to ask him the time. The bearing-down metal of the southbound train. South, Domingo thought, the train was going south.

Death had tempted his father like a sudden religion, come wearing a shirt of fire. Domingo pictured the expression on Papi's face as he flew onto the subway tracks, flew high and unwaveringly and believing—what? Everything Domingo had done since had been filtered through that look.

Papi had taught him that the worst sin for a Chinese son was to neglect his dead ancestors. Domingo remembered the story of his great-grandfather, who'd hidden in the woods after escaping the sugar plantation. When his mother had died in China, her ghost had crossed the Pacific, soared over the Rockies and the Great Plains and down the humid thumb of Florida to Cuba, looking for her son. She'd become a jungle owl and followed Chen Pan for nearly a year, fussing and hooting and disrupting his sleep. She'd even made him stop casting a shadow.

Could this, Domingo wondered, happen to him? He lit a joint and watched the shadow of his hand cupping the flame. If there was no shadow, he reasoned, there'd be no body and he'd be dead.

Domingo leaned against a sandbag and examined the barrel of his rifle. He hadn't used it much, giving away ammunition to his more trigger-happy buddies. Besides, his ears bled whenever he shot it off. His biggest fear was that in the heat of a firefight, his fellow soldiers would mistake him for a Viet Cong and shoot him dead. Enough of them were suspicious of him to begin with. With his heavy accent and brown skin, how could he be American?

In Cuba, nobody ever asked him where he was from. If you lived in Guantánamo, you were usually from there, several generations back. Everyone knew who you were. That didn't necessarily mean they were nice. Domingo's childhood nemesis, Héctor Ruíz, used to taunt him, saying his Chinese eyes tilted everything he saw. Domingo was smaller than Héctor, but he fought him every time. Now he wondered whether Héctor wasn't right all along: that his world was intrinsically askew.

Tonight the lieutenant had canceled the regular helicopter so as not to call attention to their jungle camp. Why stir up unnecessary dust? To him, choppers were good only for bringing in ammunition and food or hauling the men out when things got nasty. The lieutenant wanted everyone lying low, too, despite the pressure from headquarters to pile up enemy casualties. The men were grateful for the lieutenant's good sense. Nothing worse, Domingo agreed, than an officer who actually liked his job. Same went for squad leaders and grunts.

So far, Domingo had been lucky. In May he'd stormed into a temple with two soldiers and found a wrinkled monk bent in prayer, his teeth wired to a statue of the Buddha loaded with explosives. Domingo was standing a few feet away when the monk blew up, but he barely got scratched. After that everyone took it as fact that he was freak lucky, his instincts antennae-fine.

Domingo had had so many close calls—the dud hand grenade that had landed at his feet, the malfunctioning booby trap, the sniper's bullet deflected off the rim of his helmet—that other soldiers began clinging to him like plastic wrap. It got so nobody dared cross a rice paddy dike without checking with him. Domingo kept his great-grandfather's spectacles in a buttoned-up pocket of his flak jacket. He suspected that they were his charm.

But how long his luck would last was a matter of heavy speculation. Lester Gentry, who'd been a runner for his bookie father in Brooklyn, took odds out on Domingo every day. Domingo even placed bets on himself now and then. If, in fact, he was invincible, he wanted some of the action. A month ago Lester had machine-gunned an old woman and two little boys in their hut, the rice still warm in their bowls. Since then, Lester distracted himself by betting on how long Domingo would live.

Last week Domingo and he had managed to capture

a VC, hands up, along with his Russian pistol, some salted eggplant, and a twelve-year-old French pornographic magazine. Upon closer inspection, they found that the prisoner was barely fifteen, stringy-chested and half eaten by fire ants. He'd been living underground for a year, he confessed in his fractured English, crouched in the dark. A paperback of inspirational verse by Ho Chi Minh was stuffed in his back pocket.

Domingo had climbed into the boy-soldier's hole and felt oddly at home there. He'd found a few scraps of paper covered with poems. One was called "Nuóc," "Water," which he knew also meant "country." He'd wanted to keep the poems, maybe translate them in his spare time. But the lieutenant had ordered him to turn them in with the maps and other military debris. Domingo liked to imagine Army code breakers racking their brains trying to make sense of a Vietnamese love poem.

The rain began suddenly, igniting a soft rustle in the trees. The mountains murmured in the distance. Domingo took off his helmet, still tied with branches from the afternoon's patrol. The damn thing distorted every sound, felt like a block of concrete on his head. He was dead tired and sweating heavily.

Between the humping and the night watches,

Domingo hardly slept. At least it was better than dying unconscious. When his time came, he was determined to meet death head-on. If he were really lucky, maybe some distant relative would kill him. He'd heard that Chinese advisers were all over the VC. Still, he hated the theatricality of dying here. The sudden, light-suspended buoyancy. The senseless grace of blood. Shins protruding from mud-stuck boots. The colorful mess of intestines. Who'd told him that men killed whatever it was they came to fear?

When Domingo had gone for R&R to China Beach, he'd slept solidly for five days. He'd skipped the surf and the steaks and the whores, mostly rousing himself to drink pineapple juice and pee. In the evenings, he'd smoked Buddha weed or a little raw opium until his brain uncoiled sufficiently to sleep some more. His dreams were hazy and oranged, like rotting film. He couldn't remember a single one, only their persistent grinding light.

All the men there had just wanted to get back to the World. One guy from Arkansas fantasized about dying in his sleep, his family gathered around him, loudly grieving; a rosy, erotic death with pinup angels escorting him to heaven, sucking his dick along the way. Domingo didn't understand this hunger to grow old, this clinging to life as though anyone owned it outright. Besides, who would want to live so long when you could die dancing or go up in flames?

His last night at China Beach, Domingo had hung out by the jukebox with the black Marines, drumming along on the tables and doing his Otis Redding imitation ("I'm a Changed Man," "Groovin' Time"). Then he'd returned to the jungle, refreshed, for another killing round.

Domingo looked out at the damp horizon, imagined death coming toward him from the trees. He pressed his thumbs on his eyelids and willed himself to see in the dark, like the vampire bats in the caves outside Guantánamo. It was rumored that the bats stuck themselves to the jugulars of sleeping horses and cows, guzzling their meals of blood. *One wing soot, one wing death,* the *guajiros* would say.

After all these months, what could he believe anymore? What could never happen happened every day. Men blown out like matches. A split second cleaved living from oblivion. Once in the interrogation hut, Domingo saw the lieutenant plunge a knife into a prisoner's thigh and slash him down to his knee. He still got no answers. The prisoner was old, in his forties, lean as a kite. The old ones, everyone said, were the hardest to break.

Now all Domingo knew was this relentless feeding of death, as if feeding it were a specialty of the poor, like playing the congas or tending water buffalo. In-country, the motto was simple: *There it is.*

Last Christmas Eve his platoon had gotten caught in a firefight outside Pleiku. Six men had died in five minutes. It'd been raining so hard and out of season that their socks had rotted inside their boots. The sun had been off brooding in Cambodia. Leeches had feasted everywhere. Domingo's feet had festered so badly he could've scraped off his soles with a finger-nail.

He remembered the Christmas celebrations when he was a kid, the pig roasting in the open pit, the fat dribbling from under the crackling skin. *Noche Buena.* After the Revolution, pork was hard to come by and people made do with scrawny chickens and yams. Only Mamá hadn't seemed to mind. She was the first to volunteer for everything, cutting sugar-cane until her hands blistered and her ankles swelled with chigger bites. She never forgave Domingo for going fishing with his father on the first anniversary of the Revolution. Instead of joining the parade of his classmates with their paper flags, he'd sat by the Río Guaso waiting for the tarpon to bite.

When Papi had been arrested on charges of anti-revolutionary activities, Mamá had refused to come to his defense. She'd testified against him, reporting that he'd trafficked in contraband (a few packs of cigarettes here, a case of condensed milk there, just enough to get him in trouble). Then state security agents had tried to recruit him, but Papi refused to help. (Everyone knew that there were insurgents in the Escambray Mountains, plots to kill El Comandante, a flourishing black market in foreign weapons.) And so he was sent to the psychiatric hospital in Santiago.

Domingo had hated visiting him at the asylum. Patients caterwauled out the windows and defecated in the hallways. They bludgeoned each other with their plastic food trays. In his father's ward, rusted buckets overflowed with vomit and shit. It was no secret that his wing of the hospital was dedicated to political prisoners, although a few lunatics were sifted in for appearances' sake. Most of the men were ordinary, like Papi, except for their hatred of El Comandante. It was this that had qualified them for special revolutionary treatment: psychotropic drugs, electroshock therapy, beatings by the criminally insane released in their ward.

After a year, Papi became fixated with a yellow warbler that bathed in a puddle beneath his window. He was convinced that the bird was his grandfather, Chen Pan, returning to warn him of "everywhere evil." Mostly, Papi sat under the sapodilla tree in the courtyard, watching the pearly trails of the striped snails and talking to himself in Chinese.

Once, Domingo showed up at the hospital and

found his father strapped to his bed, his arms and legs swollen, his temples burned from electrodes. His sheets were drenched with blood and urine, and a river of saliva poured from his mouth instead of words.

"Part of his treatment," the attending nurse snapped.

No one bothered telling Domingo anything more.

A thick mist twisted down from the mountains, stifling the usual anthem of jungle noises. There was no breeze, no echo to Domingo's own cough. Normally a silence this complete would have jolted every last man in the platoon awake, but everyone continued to sleep soundly. Domingo wondered whether he could ever return home to the life before this war. But he suspected that it was too late to go back the way he had come.

Earlier in the evening, Joey Szczurak had kept Domingo company. Joey was a compulsive talker, an insomniac pill popper from Queens. He carried his P-38 can opener on a gold chain around his throat, right next to his crucifix, and charged anyone who'd lost theirs a cigarette to use his. He claimed he'd won an elocution medal at twelve, had tried heroin at fourteen.

Joey was the skinniest person Domingo had ever seen, skinnier even than Mick Jagger. His face was raw with acne. Joey's parents had lived in Warsaw during World War II. They'd begged their son not to go to Vietnam, but Joey had dropped out of Fordham and enlisted. It bothered Domingo that Joey thought nothing of unbuttoning his fatigues and masturbating to the memory of his mother's seamed stockings, his sperm arcing into the moldering sandbags.

Domingo remembered his own mother in her militia uniform, marching off to fight in the Bay of Pigs. People said that she'd killed a man, shot a *gusano* in the back who'd tried to escape. There'd been a parade for Mamá and the other veterans when they returned to Guantánamo, followed by a luncheon with the governor. Domingo had asked his mother about the shooting. Mamá's face had strained the way he'd seen it do during her more difficult deliveries, when she'd chain-smoked cigars and flung herbs in every direction. But she hadn't answered him.

The rain stopped as abruptly as it had begun. The trees were drenched and tremulant. They looked sheepish somehow, as though they'd overindulged in the storm. Domingo wished there were someone he could speak to in Spanish, but there was only that wiry Puerto Rican kid from New Jersey who missed his *arroz con gandulas*. Domingo was losing a lot of his Spanish, forgetting all his marine biology. Polyps. Holothurians. Gorgonians. The curses he still remembered. He guessed they'd be the last to go.

Domingo considered the enemy, imagined them speaking to him in Spanish, fast and with a Cuban accent, hardly an "s" every hundred words. They would tell him things—like how the wildflowers in Vietnam had changed colors from one spring to the next or how the river fish were bloating pink with chemicals, the hills wearied to nothing by napalm. In-country, Domingo had seen newborn deformities stranger than the ones in Guantánamo, infants in the central highland's villages, their features monstrously shuffled, their mothers stick-dry from weeping. *When bad things happen to the land, bad things happen to the people.* His Tío Eutemio had told him that.

When Domingo was a boy, he'd loved hiking into the mountains with his uncle to cut wood for new drums. The moon had to be full *para que no le cayeran bichos,* to keep the insects at bay. Cedar was the best and most durable, but *guásima* and mahogany, when they could find it, were also acceptable. The skins came from billy goats because the drums were *cosa de hombres.* White or yellow goats that had proven their fertility were best.

Tío Eutemio would examine the goatskins for imperfections (to avoid dead spots), then soak them in water with charcoal before scraping them clean with bricks. He always tested the skin's *tantán,* its vibe. He had an infallible ear. Tío Eutemio used to tune all the drums in the same corner of the house, the only place he "found" the sounds.

A fresh swell of mist seemed to aim at Domingo specifically. Around him, the air was thickening with ash and other detritus. He watched it, smelled it, committed it to memory, as if he knew he would have to describe it in minute detail. A dead parrot dropped out of the sky, nicking his elbow. The sweat turned cold on his back. Maybe, Domingo thought, the moon was just having a bad night.

He leveled his gun at the racing fog. His heart was audible to him, loud and fast as an all-out *descarga.* Domingo recalled how in his first month in the jungle, his platoon had come upon the rotting carcass of an elephant, its hide puckered and gray. Killed, no doubt, by starving VC. The squad leader had cried, "Ambush!" but no enemies had jumped from behind the trees. There was only this: the slow suck of the earth reabsorbing the blood and inedible muscle.

Domingo dropped his gun and stood up to receive the fog. A flare bloomed beyond the tree line. Cinders were everywhere now, as if the air itself were on fire. Whatever it was, Domingo decided, he would absorb it, become one with it, like the receiving earth.

Just then the screeching began, tortured and other-worldly. Monkeys, dozens of them, pale and dusty, with slick red throats, clambered over the foxholes, their heads large as gourds. They tore off Domingo's flak jacket, grabbed his rifle, scratched and bit his shoulders. The men bolted up in their foxholes, bug-eyed terrified, setting off wild rounds of gunfire and haphazard grenades that remarkably killed no one. The air was choked with sulfur and smoke.

They were white, those monkeys, yellow-eyed albinos—*like paunchy old men in pancake makeup*—was how Domingo described them later to the disbelieving major. What'd happened had nothing to do with reasonable explanations or the military's misplaced trust in precision (Domingo was no fan of logic himself). Yet the officers assumed that any experience could be summed up with a handful of right-angled nouns.

"We'll give you another day to rethink your story," the major said, snapping his folder shut.

Domingo thought the man looked like an oversized bullfrog.

"Sir, there won't be any changes."

The monkeys had disappeared as quickly as they'd attacked, Domingo stated for the record. They'd left footprints everywhere. An anarchy of red-fire prints. The men had tried to hunt the monkeys down, but they were nowhere to be found.

Domingo knew that the monkeys were real. He knew this because they'd torn off his flak jacket and run off with his rifle. *Coño,* the monkeys had scratched and bitten him so badly, his arms looked like ripped sleeves. He'd had to return to China Beach to get a tetanus shot. Why didn't the major check the record for himself?

"Take a look at this!" Domingo showed the major his thumb, still purple and swollen from the attack. One of the monkeys, he said, had tried to bite off his finger. "Now you tell me, sir, who the hell could make this shit up?"

TRAVELING
THROUGH
THE FLESH

I only perceive
the strange idea of family
traveling through the flesh.

      —CARLOS DRUMMOND

      DE ANDRADE

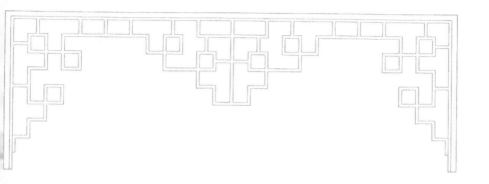

A Delicate Luck

HAVANA
(1888)

It was Good Friday, and all around the city people were pounding on boards and boxes to demonstrate their grief. *Boom-tak-tak-a-tak*. It was the one day of the year the church bells didn't ring. Lucrecia wanted to hammer on wood, too, nail the worst of her memories to a cross. Maybe then she'd finally be rid of them.

Today she had promised to help Chen Pan at the Lucky Find. In the afternoon he was bringing over furnishings from the estate of the widow Doña Dulce María Gándara, who'd lived alone in her Vedado mansion for forty years. There was a carved mahogany bed, velvet-lined boxes filled with silverware, and an extensive collection of Belgian lace. Lucrecia had an uneasy premonition about Doña Dulce María's belongings. What would they disclose? Often she could discern the history of an object by closely listening to it. Violence and unhappiness, she'd learned, seeped into things more tenaciously than the gentler emotions.

Lucrecia didn't like working on Good Friday, not because the priests had warned that it was a mortal sin (this would have no effect on Chen Pan) but because she was afraid it might invite disapproval from their neighbors and customers. Lucrecia always wore an evil eye on a chain around her neck and burned candles to clear the air of ill intention. After so many years, she was still superstitious about her own good fortune.

It made her laugh to remember how she'd mistrusted Chen Pan at first. Tall *chino* all groomed and sweet-smelling. Fingernails clean. No pigtail. Nothing like the other Chinese she'd seen—men with baskets of fruits and vegetables on poles, speaking Spanish like they were swallowing water. Men who sat in doorways, wearing pajamas and smoking long wooden pipes. Except for his eyes and his accent,

Chen Pan had looked like any other wealthy criollo in the street.

At the time Lucrecia had seen only how Chen Pan looked at her son greedily, as though he could eat him for breakfast. (She'd heard that *chinos* feasted on newborns in winter.) He'd made her so nervous that she'd almost refused to go with him. Then she'd spotted Sister Asunción on a balcony of the convent, waving her on. Lucrecia thought of her words, how God had secret plans. So she followed Chen Pan and kept her suspicions to herself.

What didn't she love about Chen Pan now? The way he drank his soup, holding the bowl with both hands and bringing it to his lips. The passion with which he recited his father's poems in Chinese. The fact that he smiled only when he meant it. How he sank his face into her hair when they made love.

Lucrecia pulled the feather duster from its rusty hook and started on the items in the window. She rather liked the candelabra with its six brass peacocks. Next to it was a mannequin in full livery and spats. An alabaster statue of a nude woman occupied a pedestal by the front door. Lucrecia detested the smug expression on her face, like those of the women in church who reclined on their Oriental rugs while their servants knelt behind them on the stone floor.

Chen Pan had asked Lucrecia to make room for the

widow's things, but how could anything more fit in their shop? He would be irritable, too, if she got rid of so much as a teacup.

The door bell jingled as two women in matching dresses entered the Lucky Find. They were twins, their faces shiny as new fruit. Lilac corsages were pinned to their bosoms.

"Are you looking for something special, *señoras?*" Lucrecia asked.

The light was dim, and she could tell that the women were trying to gauge the precise shade of her skin. They weren't accustomed to seeing *mulatas* in the finer shops. The sisters barely moved their lips, and Lucrecia had trouble deciphering who was speaking.

"Do you have monkeys?" one of them inquired.

Lucrecia led the ladies to an adjoining alcove where the decorative animals were stored. She was partial to a miniature hippopotamus, which she thought looked like an amiable cross between a pig and a cow.

The sisters hunted the shelves stealthily, as if they might sneak up on their prey. They admired a hand-painted lamb and shuddered before a woodcut of a leopard. But there were no monkeys. As they turned to go, Lucrecia spotted one of the sisters slipping a crystal frog into a fold of her dress.

If this had been the street, Lucrecia might have wrestled the woman to the ground to reclaim her merchandise (the other peddlers would have rallied to her assistance). Instead she bent over, pretending to pick up something off the floor, and emitted the unmistakable trill of a frog. *Brrriii, brrriii.* Once, twice, three times it took for the woman to release the frog and tuck it under a chair cushion.

Lucrecia resumed her dusting with vigor. The glass case under Chen Pan's abacus was devoted to religious articles: prayer books and crucifixes, two chalices and a bishop's miter, rosaries of varying lengths and hues. One worn blue rosary had been there for years. It reminded Lucrecia of her mother's hands, of the African sayings she'd made her memorize. *Aseré ebión beromo, itá maribá ndié ekrúkoro.* When the sun comes out, it shines on everyone. *Champompón champompón ñanga dé besoá.* What was yesterday is not today.

Mamá had been devoted to Yemayá, goddess of the seas. She used to dress Lucrecia in blue and white and together they'd take offerings to the beach on Sundays, coconut balls or fried pork rinds when she could make them. They'd lived with an evil couple on Calle San Juan de Dios. Mamá had done everything for them—cooked their meals over the charcoal fire, polished the marble floors, washed and ironed their sheets every day. She'd put Lucrecia to work boiling the master's handkerchiefs, which were always so *mocosos* they'd made her gag.

The master used to visit her mother every night.

Mamá would cover Lucrecia with a sheet, teach her to still her breathing. A terrible pig-groaning, the bed shuddering with fleas, then the master would leave for another day. Lucrecia had believed that this was just another of her mother's chores, like washing clothes or peeling yams. Mamá stuffed rags that smelled of sour milk between her legs. She never explained anything.

Boom *tak-tak-a-tak.* All morning long, the penitents banged on their wood. In Havana, everyone suffered as hard as they played. Early on Ash Wednesday, Lucrecia had seen people wear *cenizas* on their foreheads, but by noon they were eating meat and trading horses. Last year, a Dutch nun had told her that Cubans were immoral. Where else was it normal for a priest to go straight from church to the cock pit without bothering to remove his three-cornered hat? And the priests had families of their own with mistresses on the side, just like any other man.

After the Protestant missionaries gave up on Chen Pan, they concentrated on converting Lucrecia. "From what?" she'd ask, serving them *cafesito* with guava and cheese. They told her that she was living in sin, that she had to marry Chen Pan to sit right in the eyes of God. One sermon after another. Lucrecia knew that what they said had nothing to do with her.

If she believed anything, it was this: Whenever you helped someone else, you saved yourself. Isn't that what Chen Pan had done when he'd taken her from Don Joaquín?

In her opinion it was better to mix a little of this and that, like when she prepared an *ajiaco* stew. She lit a candle here, made an offering there, said prayers to the gods of heaven and the ones here on earth. She didn't believe in just one thing. Why would she eat only ham croquettes? Or enjoy the scent of roses alone? Lucrecia liked to go to church on Easter to admire the *flores de pascuas,* but did she need to go every Sunday?

Chen Pan, on the other hand, grew more inflexible with age. Lately, he'd begun insisting on Chinese-only explanations for everything: such as that everyone was born with *yuan,* a destiny inherited from previous lives; or that the earth balanced on the back of a giant turtle; or—she found this most silly—that everyone who wasn't Chinese was a ghost.

Lucrecia sighed as she refolded a silk tablecloth. The enormous Spanish armoire was bulging with brocaded curtains, yards of fraying linen, and clothing at least fifty years old in dire need of cleaning. None of it sold particularly well (except to one spindly antiques dealer from New York) and spent years moldering on the shelves. After a time, no amount of fresh air or beating could rid it of its mustiness.

Although Lucrecia kept a few candles for sale at the Lucky Find, she sold most of her wares on the street. *¡Cómpreme las velas pa' evitar las peleas!* Buy my candlelight to avoid bitter fights! This wasn't exactly true but it was difficult to find a good rhyme for *velas*. And a catchy *pregón* attracted people like a bad accident. What tickled Lucrecia—and Chen Pan, too—was that her customers claimed that the candles actually brought peace to their homes.

From the start, Lucrecia had loved everything about making candles. The scent of the hot wax in the cauldrons. How it cooled so pure and smooth on the wicks. The way the candles burned in church, shrinking swiftly and painlessly, as she imagined a good life would. Lucrecia once heard a French prioress say that the churches in Havana burned more candles in a month than the churches in Paris did all year long. And Paris, she'd claimed, was many times the size of Havana.

Lucrecia kept her money in an account at the Chinese bank on Calle Zanja. She'd opened the account after Chen Pan had gone off to deliver machetes to Commander Sian. Little by little, she deposited her profits there. A year after Chen Pan returned from the war, Lucrecia gave him the seven hundred pesos she'd saved to buy her freedom. He took the money. What choice did he have? He knew she couldn't have loved him otherwise. But instead of leaving, Lucrecia told Chen Pan that if it pleased him, she preferred to stay.

It was a Sunday in May when they first made love. Very early, before dawn. Lucrecia went to Chen Pan in her sky-blue dressing gown, midnight dropping her blossoms. He reached for her like the edge of heaven. Then a heat and longing grew between them, a joy so strong and unknown they laughed and cried together.

Lucrecia polished a silver platter and thought of the children they'd had since. Desiderio was born all fire, nine pounds of squalling flame. He was dangerously handsome, too—a woman's lips, hair sleeked back with perfume, lured by each and every risk. Lorenzo was less flamboyant. His hair was thick and cottony, and his feet were identical to hers. And Caridad was born with a spot at the base of her spine that Chen Pan said made her truly Chinese. She was pretty and fine-boned and sang like the lovebirds they peddled on the Plaza de Armas.

Lucrecia suspected that Chen Pan loved Lorenzo best. By the time their son was nine years old, he was treating all kinds of ailments. Chen Pan put him to study with the herbal master from F——, whose specialty was curing consumption. (A month of the doctor's foul-smelling plasters, and his patients stopped coughing forever.) Last December, Lorenzo had left to study medicine in China. Lucrecia hadn't seen Chen Pan so heartbroken since they'd lost Víctor Manuel.

Every day, she prayed to the Buddha and to all the saints to keep Lorenzo safe.

I t was nearly lunchtime and Chen Pan hadn't returned from Doña Dulce María's place. Had the widow's sons decided against surrendering their mother's possessions? A change of heart was not uncommon in this business. A month ago, Lucrecia had accompanied Chen Pan to a retired general's home—he'd promised to sell them his collection of international swords—only to have him threaten them both with beheading should they cross his threshold.

Their own apartment hadn't changed much since Lucrecia had moved to Calle Zanja twenty years ago. There were no luxuries, no silver or porcelain plates to break. Everything was sturdy and useful, like Chen Pan himself. In the kitchen was an altar with a statue of a fat *chino* sitting cross-legged and content. Her first day there, Lucrecia had offered the Buddha a sprig of mint that she'd worn tucked in her bosom to keep her milk plentiful. What else did she have to give?

Chen Pan had tried to teach her how to eat with chopsticks, but Lucrecia couldn't balance them on her fingertips. She was accustomed to eating leftovers, a bit of rice or burnt *malanga,* a scrap of jerked beef now and then. She always used her hands. For a long time, Lucrecia had only pretended to sleep as she waited for Chen Pan's attack. Of course, it never came.

To remember all this made Lucrecia sad and happy at once—sad, because she hadn't recognized Chen Pan's kindness; happy, because his kindness hadn't lessened over the years. What would have become of her life if Chen Pan hadn't opened the newspaper that day long ago? Sometimes, Lucrecia thought, survival depended on the most delicate luck.

Her mother hadn't been so fortunate. She'd died from yellow fever—black vomit for days, a stench Lucrecia could still smell. Mamá hadn't been buried a month when Don Joaquín went to see her. He lifted her nightshirt, spread her legs, jammed a finger inside her. Then he licked his finger slowly. "You're ready, *puta,*" he said, undoing his pants, and pushed himself on her. When Lucrecia cried out, he hit her. His ring bruised her cheek, made her nose bleed. Then he covered her mouth and finished his business.

It took Lucrecia many years to realize that she was his daughter (her resemblance to him was unmistakable). That what her mother had suffered, she was now suffering. That Mamá had loved her in spite of her hatred for him. That Yemayá had helped them survive.

Ay, Sagrada Virgen, Señora de Regla,
dame tu fuerza y protégenos de nuestros
enemigos . . .

Once, when Lucrecia dared to call him Papá, Don Joaquín choked her so hard she stopped breathing. She saw flashes of white, then nothing at all. He slapped her awake. "Say that again and I'll grind up your bones and sell you as pig feed." It didn't stop him from battering her harder that night.

From then on, the master made her keep her eyes open when he did it, made her watch his beastly face. He hit her if she blinked, made her repeat things she never since said aloud. For years, Lucrecia stopped dreaming. Everything inside her stayed tight and kneeling, waiting day after day, holding her breath like Mamá had taught her.

At one o'clock, Lucrecia closed the shop and climbed the stairs to their apartment. That morning she'd killed a chicken by whipping it around like a windmill until she'd broken its neck. Then she'd ground its meat into a paste for soup. Now she heated a spoonful of lard in her heaviest skillet and quickly chopped two onions. She peeled and minced several cloves of garlic, stirred them in the fat, and added yesterday's bread crumbs.

Lucrecia remembered how Don Joaquín had refused to eat anything but steak. When he'd finally banished her to the convent, how relieved she'd been! It was cool there, not hot and sooty like in the mistress's kitchen. It was agreed that Lucrecia would stay with the nuns until her baby came, until the master could sell them both. Unbaptized, unschooled, and cursed as she was, the sisters received her and took her to church. The priest swung a shiny gold censer that released clouds of smoke. It smelled to Lucrecia like a thousand dying flowers.

As her baby grew and fattened inside her, Lucrecia dipped hundreds of candles in the bubbling vats. Long white tapers for Sunday mass and society weddings. Thick ivory ones for the sacristy. Pastels for the various feast days. Gilded votives for La Virgen de la Caridad del Cobre, Cuba's patron saint. For Good Friday, the nuns fashioned candles darkened with tar. *To burn away the sins of the world.*

Boom-tak-tak-a-tak. *Boom tak-tak-a-tak.* The banging in the street was growing louder, more insistent, as if all her neighbors had taken up grieving. Lucrecia finished the chicken soup and went back downstairs to the Lucky Find.

There was a customer waiting out front with a face like one of Chen Pan's old maps. Lucrecia let him in, but she didn't understand a word he said. Was he trying to speak Spanish? Usually she could tell which language a foreigner spoke by his accent, but this sounded like nothing she'd heard before. She motioned for the customer to look around, pointing to the items she guessed might interest him: the gilded cuckoo clock, the rosewood vanity set, the solid silver candlesticks.

Finally, she deciphered his painstaking introduction. He was a *taxidermista* from Poland! Lucrecia laughed and shook her head. She was tempted to say that there were several of Chen Pan's friends—rare specimens indeed—that she might recommend for immediate stuffing. Instead she informed the man that he'd come to the wrong address.

The remainder of the afternoon was quiet. Lucrecia grew restless. She needed to place an ad for her lantern candles. They were popular during the spring festival, and she liked to advertise in advance. Besides, it gave her an opportunity to go to the Chinese newspaper's offices on Calle San Nicolás. There she watched the men pull the tiny blocks of characters from the thousands on display. Later she would stare at the headlines and coax Chen Pan to say them aloud, repeating them until she learned a phrase or two.

But Chen Pan had no patience to teach her Chinese. The little that Lucrecia had absorbed she'd picked up in the streets, or from her friend Esperanza Yu. It wasn't always polite. Lucrecia had relished the alarm on Chen Pan's face when she'd come home with a few choice obscenities. Other *cubanos* who had business in Chinatown also learned some Chinese. Like her, they spoke a kind of *chino-chuchero*.

When she'd moved to Calle Zanja, no business had been as prosperous as Chen Pan's. Today there were groceries and hotels, pharmacies, bakeries, and gambling dens—even two Buddhist pagodas. And everyone knew the Chinese made the best ice cream in Havana. On Sundays people came from everywhere to buy it.

It was true that she could go shopping in the Mercado de Cristina or at the fancy stores on Calle Obispo, buy muslins and ribbons at St. Anthony's or a three-layer cake at Goddess Diana. But what need did she have for such frills? Everything she loved was in Chinatown. The tamales with smoked duck. The fried sweet potatoes, finely chopped. Her favorite dessert was also Chinese—a pound cake with so many sesame seeds it was called *chino con piojos,* Chinaman with fleas.

She was a part of Chinatown now, at peace here, with the smells and sounds she'd once found so foreign. How could she think of baking chicken without plenty of ginger? Or deciding something important without offering persimmons to the Buddha? Lucrecia had encouraged her children to learn Chinese, too, but only Lorenzo showed any interest.

Last fall, she and her son had gone to the Chinese theater on Calle Salud. It was beautiful, painted like Christmas in red and gold. There were acrobats from Shanghai who climbed on each other's shoulders and flew through the air like show-off birds. Singers in satin costumes wailed of lost love and the bittersweet gifts of spring. And the music was a clang of cymbals and drums that couldn't have been more different from the Cuban *danzón*.

At four o'clock, a gigantic carriage pulled up in front of the Lucky Find. Chen Pan pointed to the loaded cart behind him. "We'll have to take over the shop next door!" he laughed, loud enough for the whole neighborhood to hear.

Sometimes Lucrecia questioned the origin of her birth, but she didn't question who she'd become. Her name was Lucrecia Chen. She was thirty-six years old and the wife of Chen Pan, mother of his children. She was Chinese in her liver, Chinese in her heart.

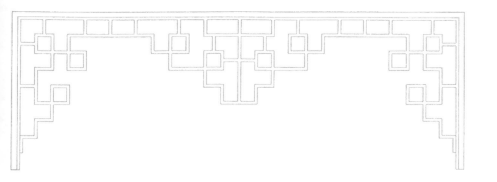

Plums

Chen Fang

SHANGHAI
(1939)

I had been teaching for nearly twelve years when I met Dauphine de Moët. She was the mother of three boys at our school. Her children were escorted everywhere by a pair of White Russian body-guards. Kidnapping was rampant in Shanghai—it has always been something of a local specialty—but those were extraordinary measures a decade ago.

Dauphine's husband, Charles de Moët, was a French businessman and former diplomat. He'd speculated in the Shanghai stock market and invested in a leather factory that later made army boots for the Japanese invaders. The de Moëts lived in a French Concession mansion with many antiques and a full-time staff. Once I saw D—— leave their house. He was the gangster who terrorized Shanghai.

Dauphine invited me to tea to review the boys' grades, which were less than satisfactory. It was a Sunday, and Dauphine answered the door herself. I noticed her thick hands as she poured the rare jasmine tea. There were sweetmeats wrapped in crimson paper and miniature cakes oozing cream. Dauphine wore a silk tunic cut in the Chinese style. Her long blond hair hung like a voyage.

She watched my every gesture, the uncertainty of my lips as I formed the words to speak. She told me that I was beautiful. Nobody had ever said this to me before. I felt a heat rise to my cheeks.

Dauphine had a wonderful library of books and allowed me to borrow whatever I wished. She also liked to paint and showed me a watercolor she'd done of a piebald charger that was quite delicately rendered. It galloped toward the viewer as though it would fly off the paper. Her other paintings were not as good, but still rich with poetic intent.

I was invited to tea many times that winter of

1928. The months were brutally cold, lashed by unforgiving winds. My visits were the same: an empty house, the steaming tea, Dauphine's gentle attentiveness. Sometimes she wore a crystal necklace that caught the faint winter light, or a scarf double-tied at her waist.

Dauphine told me she'd grown up in Alsace-Lorraine hating the Germans. For two years she'd also lived in Brazil, where she sailed the Amazon and once watched piranhas eat a horse to the bone.

Her husband had been the French consul general in Havana during the Great War. It was the time of the Dance of the Millions, she explained, when Cubans made overnight fortunes in sugar. Palaces lined the boulevards, and fancy cars cruised up and down the city's seawall. She said that the Cubans, like the Spaniards, used a spice in their rice that turned it the color of kumquats.

Dauphine had many photographs of Havana, including one of an old Chinese man in a doorway smoking an opium pipe. I liked to imagine that this man might have known my father or grandfather. She played Cuban records on her phonograph, too. At first the music sounded strange to me. But I grew to love the torrent of drums, the torn-sounding voices of the singers. Dauphine showed me how to dance like the Cubans, clasping me tightly and making me swing my hips.

There was a club in Old Havana, Dauphine told me, where women wore men's evening clothes and kissed each other on the lips. They drank rum punch, lit their lovers' cigars, picked their teeth clean with silver toothpicks. I knew, listening to her, that I knew nothing at all.

Occasionally, Dauphine cooked for me. Nothing lavish. Our favorite snack was toasted ham-and-cheese sandwiches—*croque monsieurs*—that she served with tiny pickles and beer. Another time, she steamed mussels in a wine broth and insisted on feeding them to me one by one.

She asked me about my life. I told her about the stone wall that encircled our mountain village to keep the bandits out. At the west end of the gorge, Mother lay beautiful as an empress in her bed, wreathed in opium smoke. One spring the musk deer ate all the leaves off the trees and the goats swelled from a mysterious disease and died. What more did I have to tell?

On my thirtieth birthday, Dauphine had her chef prepare for me the traditional longevity noodles. She knew I loved green plums and presented me with an exquisite jade bowl filled to the brim with them, although plums were long out of season.

"For my beloved Fang," Dauphine whispered as she presented me with the fruit.

"You are too kind," I answered, lowering my eyes.

That day, we became lovers.

The hardships of the times receded for me. Our lives became hidden as if in a thousand-year dream. Behind her fragrant embankment of candles, I knew only the wrinkled petals of Dauphine's eyelids, the caress of her knowing fingers, the easy laugh of her rapture. With every embrace, a tide of blood rose between us. Far from the bright censoring light, I recited for her all the love poems I had memorized as a child.

But joy, I soon learned, is only a fleeting passage from one sorrow to the next.

That autumn, Dauphine's husband took his family back to France. There was talk of markets failing, of their fortune in ruins. So much red dust. I noticed Dauphine's earrings, long and linked, the delicate chains grazing her shoulders. They were returning to Paris, she told me, to tend to their ruins.

Dauphine gave me an ivory back scratcher, her rabbitskin hat, a lock of her hair wrapped in rice paper, and, at the last moment, the painting of the piebald charger. I did not sleep for a year. My face grew sallow, my eyes filmed with ash. Where did history go, I asked myself, if it could not be retold?

I felt raw with the knowledge of pleasure, charred by it. I understood finally the truth of the Tao Te Ching:

> The reason that we have great affliction is that
>   we have bodies.
> Had we not bodies, what affliction would we
>   have?

Once in the mountains, I saw a snake shedding its skin. It began at the back of its neck, a faint split, before slowly unsheathing its yellow-brown length. In the end, the snake was still itself but somehow shinier and new.

Sometimes when I teach, I see myself in the younger girls and wonder: Will they ever learn their singular natures?

After Dauphine left, ordinary pleasures eluded me—the heat and noise of the opera, the taste of roast duck with pepper and salt, the warmth of the sun's first rays as I walked to school. I dreamed the same dream every night. A woman, not myself, is drowning in a river, the water collecting in her lungs. Her hair is long and unspools in the current. She pulls it out by the fistful until the river flows cleanly through her net of black strands.

The following summer, I found a shaman on the edge of Shanghai. For two days I watched him swirl by his fires, listening to his mournful chants until I fell into a trance. It was then I saw Dauphine again, lovely in a fresh linen dress, fishing by the bluest of rivers. I called to her, and without turning she nodded. Then she pulled a ripe plum from the water. It was raining, hard and slow, the kind of rain that lasts for days. I called to Dauphine again, and again she nodded. Her blond hair bobbed like a New Year's lantern as she caught another plum. I tried to get a closer look, but a steady wind held me in place. When I awoke, I knew I had lost her forever.

For years, my heart swung in my chest. The wind slept in my empty hands. My life lay scattered like unswept petals after a storm. I sat *ch'an* for many hours, seeking peace. Perhaps, I thought, I could become like the wise Chieh-yü, who feigned madness and lived as a recluse to avoid public service.

I grew impatient with my students. Only one in a hundred truly listened. As for the rest, I might as well have been reading to monkeys. What could I teach them, anyway? That knowledge was more important than love? (I no longer believed this.) And the pettiness of my colleagues, bickering over supplies and oversights. How could I stand to walk the dreary corridors of that school, pretending to be a teacher? Pretending tranquility?

I forced myself to consider the tentative overtures of specific men: the diminutive chemist with the withered hand; the district supervisor who sang all evening in a moving baritone. Impossibilities! Could they not see how inapt they were for me? One spurned suitor accused me: *It is always due to women's dog hearts that men are never free!*

So was this my life's allotment? To have rejoiced in one brief love?

> *My bed is so empty that I keep on waking up:*
> *As the cold increases, the night-wind begins to*
> * blow.*
> *It rustles the curtains, making a noise like the*
> * sea:*
> *Oh that those were waves which could carry me*
> * back to you!*

No doubt there was a secret language that would restore all my loss. But how was I to learn it? Again, I found the shaman and begged him to make me forget. And for a time, I did. I lived as an insect in amber, protected from memory. Little by little, though, everything returned to me in vivid wisps. Like a stubborn old woman throwing stones in the temple, I hoped for a miracle. Of course, none came. I grew used to the void again.

A few years ago, I began collecting funeral urns. I line them up along the walls of my bedroom. One of the secondhand dealers, Mr. Yi, asked me why I am so taken with ornaments of death, but I could not answer him. I thought of planting flowers in the urns, but they lack proper drainage and I cannot bear the thought of all those blooms facing a certain demise.

Often I think of my son, who will become a man soon. I had not told Dauphine about him, I do not know why. I have a son, the same age as her youngest. A boy who grew up without me. What is Chih-mo like? Is he angry with me for having abandoned him? What did his father's family tell him? Does he know I am alive?

Outside my window, the magnolia tree has not flowered. Crows fill its branches, three or four dozen at once. No spring onions are left in my flowerpots. On Saturday morning, after an all-night rain, I discovered a striped snail inching its way along my balcony. Where did it come from? How did it find its way to my few sad circles of dirt?

It is summer again. I am forty years old, the year that divides a woman's life in two. Before this, one

can be considered pretty. There is hope of more children. A bit of vanity is still permitted. Afterward, it is
unseemly to take pains with one's appearance. A husband lingers less on his wife's body, hurrying his
pleasure, or if he's rich enough, bestows his ardor on a
new concubine.

A woman's second season is long and bitter. Satisfaction comes in arranging a good marriage for her
son, fetching a fair bride price for her daughter. I say
this, but my life is not a woman's life. I live like a
man, like less than a man, alone in my two rooms.

The hospitable years are over. The Japanese are
everywhere. Flags with their red savage suns flutter
on every rooftop. The city is stripped down and starving, the fields around us all husks and wind. Only the
same pack of dogs is fat from feasting on corpses.

It is said that there are no more poppies in the
fields, that the water is unsafe to drink, contaminated
by the dead. Others say that in places the rain comes
down black with revenge. A mere trickle of water
escapes my faucets. I put my cooking pots on the balcony to catch the rain, then boil it for an hour before
drinking it. I carry this water in bottles to school. Once
a week, I collect enough rain to take a bath.

I have not been paid in months. How I live day to
day, I cannot say. I go from home to school, from
school to the market and home again. At the market,
there is not much to buy: wilted cabbages, an ounce or

two of dried noodles. I make simple soups with what is available, or mix a bit of tofu with rice. I keep potato flour and sesame oil on hand for extra flavoring. Mostly, all food tastes the same to me.

In the evenings I correct my students' papers, prepare tea, and read for hours. Reading is my one luxury. It does not save me from want, nor will it free me from death. Certainly, it prevents me from getting a full night's sleep. But immersed in the shadows of other worlds, I find a measure of peace.

When I cannot concentrate, I stand on my balcony and watch the moon. It shines alone in skies clear or clouded, illuminating nothing. I remember watching this same moon as a girl in the mountains. Once I had imagined it to be a magic pearl that would grant all my wishes. But what did I know then to desire?

In China they say the greatest glory for a woman is to bear and raise sons for the future. So where, I ask, is my place? I am neither woman nor man but a stone, a tree struck by lightning long ago. Everything that has followed since counts for nothing.

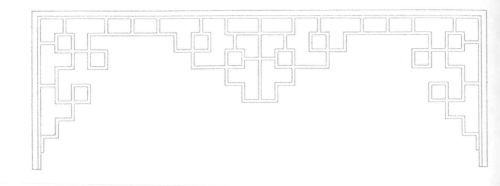

Small World

SAIGON
(1970)

D omingo Chen was released from the hospital just in time to turn twenty. His belt buckle scraped his gut where the shrapnel had torn him up a month after he'd signed up for his second tour of duty. The land mine had claimed four limbs from three different men. He'd lost only a clump of his intestines, the smoothness of his hairless chest, and the brand-new tattoo—a reproduction of a Santa Bárbara prayer card—that he'd gotten on R&R in China Beach.

Actually, he hadn't lost the tattoo entirely. Bits of green and red still flecked his scars with a dull glitter. A tilted eye had knit itself below his left nipple, a minuscule hand gesticulated above his navel, waving wildly whenever he laughed. His great-grandfather's spectacles had survived intact, but whatever luck they'd imparted obviously had run out. When the gunships had flown in to retaliate for the mine, Domingo had watched trees, roots and all, somersaulting through the air.

In the hospital, he'd found it difficult to follow his father's long-ago advice. *Don't watch with interest the suffering of others.* But how could he avoid it? Everywhere he looked, crisply gauzed catastrophes looked back. Maimings and head injuries and the fevered hallucinations of desperate men. He was impressed by how the mind adapted to severe pain with saving visions—the homely nurse transformed into an erotic goddess; the soldier convinced that his missing dick was a flowering cherry tree.

To pass the time, Domingo gambled with the other patients in the hospital corridors or smoked dope out the windows, courtesy of the sympathetic orderly who came around midnight with the ward's supply. Domingo was surprised at the number of black soldiers who'd been named after presidents—Washingtons and Roosevelts, Lincolns and Jeffersons. It was no different in Cuba, he supposed. Every tenth boy a little Fidel. American officers had simpler names, like John or Bill or Fred. As far as Domingo could tell, the higher the rank the vaguer their mission.

Sometimes fights broke out in the ward. Men missing an arm or a leg, restrained by pain and morphine drips, hurled syringes and urine bags, whatever was at hand, trying to finish the job the jungle hadn't. The MPs were sent in to restore order, but the sight of those whole, strong men depressed everyone. Besides, what could the MPs do? Handcuff the amputees?

The pomaded little chaplain showed up after every brawl, too. His job was to convince the men that everything was going to be okay when everyone knew for a fact that nothing would ever be right again. After all, what was left of them to save? And even if their bodies healed, their minds would go on suffering. Domingo thought the chaplain spoke in a strange compressed way, as if his sentences weighed more than anyone's. Dead men sentences. Later, Domingo never could remember what'd started the fights.

Outside the hospital, the sky threatened rain. Domingo looked up at the thickening clouds and thought of the monk from Hue, who'd drenched himself with kerosene and set himself aflame on a busy Saigon street. He'd watched the footage on Cuban television and the reports of copycat self-immolations. "Read this!" His mother had thrust the newspaper at him in disgust. "Let's see what your father says about that!" Madame Nhu, the Vietnamese president's sister-in-law, had proclaimed the rash of self-immolations a "barbecue party" and said, "Let them burn, and we shall clap our hands."

On Le Loi Street, Domingo passed a bareheaded man selling two fertilized duck eggs. Domingo knew that the eggs, boiled and salted, were a delicacy in Vietnam. He paid too much for them and carefully slid them into the pockets of his fatigues. From another vendor he bought one ripe apricot.

It was winter and the air was cold. Domingo made his way to Cholon, the Chinese district. More vendors hurried by with vegetables on bamboo poles. Others squatted behind straw mats of green bananas, sweet-sops, batteries, or cigarettes. One toothless woman had a single used book for sale.

The sound of a shrill flute drifted toward Domingo, but he couldn't determine its origin. Garbage was everywhere—decaying rinds, filthy scraps in every shade of moldering gray. Down one alley, stink fruit vines overflowed from rusty cans on a balcony. Domingo thought of how his mother used to say that all mysteries grew from dead or dying things because death was the color of everything.

Mamá had become president of the Guantánamo chapter of the Cuban Physicians in Solidarity with

Vietnam Brigade. Napalm victims were being sent to Cuba for treatment. Children missing eyes and ears and feet. When his mother had learned that Domingo was in Vietnam fighting for the Americans, she'd stopped writing to him altogether.

After the Bay of Pigs, Mamá had predicted that the Americans would invade the island again. But Papi had argued that the *yanquis* were no longer a threat. Take a look, he'd said, at what they ate: pizza and roast beef and triple fudge cake. Who could wage a war eating like that?

Papi had thought that the Revolution was far more dangerous than the United States. He used to pore over the articles about China he'd clipped since the Communists had taken over. "Millions are starving in the provinces in the name of revolutionary change. So how can we support these *descarados* in Cuba who are doing the same?" Papi had insisted that the Revolution couldn't work because it focused solely on ideas, not people. "The arrogance of El Comandante to give new names to everything! As if he could invent the future!"

Domingo's first thought when Tham Thanh Lan opened the door was that Danny Spadoto had lied. She didn't smell like coconuts at all. No, what she smelled like was that tiger balm all the Vietnamese prostitutes used to heat up a flagging cock. Tham Thanh Lan's eyes widened as if she recognized him but quickly settled back into a wary tiredness. Her mouth was full and poppy red. She seemed familiar to Domingo, like he'd known her as a child.

He'd heard all the rumors: how the whores in these parts kept broken glass in their vaginas, how they passed on incurable strains of venereal disease, how their victims were left spongy-brained and quarantined for life on South Pacific islands owned by Uncle Sam.

Domingo held up a parcel he'd meticulously wrapped with stolen hospital gauze. Tham Thanh Lan stared at it limply, as though it contained something she herself had discarded and hoped never to see again. He continued to stand there, dumbly offering his gift. He tried to smile. His teeth felt unnaturally large in his mouth.

Tham Thanh Lan took the parcel, unwound the gauze, casually considered the contents: a last picture of Danny Spadoto, chin pressing the lower limb of a kapok tree; the half-smoked cigarette Domingo had pulled from his dead lips; Danny's shiny dog tags; his high school ring with the fake ruby stone—Newark High, class of '66. She examined only the ring closely, weighed it in her hand, then slipped it into a hidden pocket of her satin pants.

"He talked to me about you," Domingo began. He wanted to say that Danny had loved her, but he wasn't sure this was true. Domingo had collected his friend's remains from the breadfruit tree and then slid him, piece by piece, into a body bag. He'd baby-sat the bag, grief-sickened, until dinnertime when the chopper flew in right on schedule to pick up the dead.

Tham Thanh Lan tried to close the door, but Domingo held it open. "Please." He tried not to whine. His heart was jumping like the times he'd climbed in the Sierra Maestra with his uncle. Tham Thanh Lan's gaze rinsed over him, took in the stubble of his newly shaven skull, his bandage-thickened middle, the bulge in his pocket suggesting a promising wad of bills.

"Where are you from?" she demanded.

"Cuba," he said. "I'm from Cuba." He was tired of explaining this to everyone.

"What happened to you?" Tham Thanh Lan's voice was pitched high and thin, like an Okónkolo drum.

Domingo didn't know where to begin—how he carried the darkness inside him now, how trampling on plants made him cringe. He wanted to talk about the forests of rubber trees he'd seen, about the elephant grass and flame vines that reminded him of Cuba. In Vietnam, he'd noticed, everything flowered all at once, not in fits and starts like deciduous New York. At what point had all this foliage turned to camouflage?

Domingo reached into his pockets and pulled out

the duck eggs, offering them to Tham Thanh Lan. He gave her the apricot, too.

Tham Thanh Lan wasted no time boiling water in an old tin pot. The steam filled the tiny apartment. Thick droplets collected on the ceiling. Domingo detected the potent aroma of fermenting fish. Tham Thanh Lan said that normally she would have let the ducks hatch and grow, but in Saigon they'd be stolen in no time. It was better to eat them right away. Then she sliced the apricot into abundance and served it on a flowered plate.

There were bits of military trash scattered on her kitchen shelves—belt buckles, canteens, a handful of spent ammunition, a helmet printed with numbers crossed off at fifty-six. On a hook in the corner hung a four-foot-long snakeskin, its yellow diamonds faded to gold. A huge, wrinkled map of Vietnam covered most of another wall, pockmarked with blots of ink. Next to it was a bed the size of a child's, narrow and neat, the sheets stained with sweat.

When the duck eggs were cooked, Tham Thanh Lan took hers and broke its soft translucent membrane. She drank the liquid, sprinkled salt and pepper on the yolk, then scooped it out with a spoon and ate it with some *thom* leaves. Domingo gave her his egg and she ate it as well.

Domingo began thinking of stories to tell her. About the time a pack of Jamaican Negresses had chased his Abuelo Lorenzo along the Bay of Santiago, determined to try his virginity powder. Or how his Tío Desiderio had owned the most notorious gambling den in Havana and kept a British pistol strapped to his calf. Or how his father had made the best shrimp dumplings in Guantánamo, maybe all of Cuba. But Domingo wasn't sure any of this would make sense to her.

Instead he pulled up his shirt and showed Tham Thanh Lan where the shrapnel had torn him up and the Army doctor had stitched him back together.

"Touch it," he said.

When she didn't, Domingo took her hand and guided it along his scars. Her nails were long and scratched him lightly. He played with her hands, delicately at first, one finger at a time, before bringing them to his lips.

The downpour shook the building, rattled the empty glass jars, made the fading snakeskin sway from its hook. The stiff little curtain billowed into the room with each gust of wind. A few storm-littered leaves drifted through the window. One moment, Tham Thanh Lan was swathed in pale satin; the next, there was only the candor of her naked flesh. Domingo's eyes hurt from trying to see all of her at once.

He thought of the whorehouse that his Tío Eutemio had taken him to when he was fourteen. The women had been dressed like geishas and schoolgirls, prison inmates, and mermaids with speckled rubber fins. The back room, it was said, had been outfitted like a medieval dungeon and offered a malnourished girl in an ancient chastity belt who was especially popular with the locksmiths in the province. For his first time, Domingo had chosen a pendulously breasted *negra* who'd reminded him of his mother.

Domingo brought his face close to Tham Thanh Lan's. Her eyes were open, but there was no curiosity in them. Her nipples were dark brown coins. Everywhere he kissed—the slight upward curve of her breasts, the length of her sinewy legs—he coaxed forth new scents. The betel nuts her father had chewed the day he'd sold Tham Thanh Lan to the passing fish sauce trader. The banana pudding she used to cook for him Sunday nights. The smell of the men who'd paid the trader a few *đồng* apiece to sleep with the girl from the North.

A seam of numbers paraded along the inside of Tham Thanh Lan's right thigh, smelling of enemy metal. She told Domingo that the numbers were the identity code of a jealous Republican general. And the scars between her legs—she opened them wide to show him—were from this same general, who had once tied her to the bed and penetrated her with his dagger. Tham Thanh Lan had been told two things in her hospital bed: that she could no longer bear children and that the general had shown up at Army headquarters and shot himself in the head.

Domingo delicately licked Tham Thanh Lan, pushing the tufts of her hair aside with his tongue. "I'm sorry," he murmured. *"Tôi nghiêp,"* he repeated in Vietnamese.

He thought of the pygmy boas that he used to spot by the Río Guaso. *Majacitos bobos.* The snakes curled up into balls and released a foul smell, squeezing blood from their eyes to scare off predators. They were supposedly benign, but people would tell you otherwise: of the cousin who fell into a trance and croaked like a frog after having been bitten; of the aunt whose thumb blackened and dropped off her hand, leaving nothing but a charred-looking stump.

Domingo was from the Río Guaso, from the grasses where the snakes lay in wait, from the palm trees where the boisterous parakeets lived, flashing the red patches beneath their wings. He'd spent his whole childhood by that river, assuming he would never leave, swimming beneath its tents of whispering trees.

Domingo burrowed his face deep between Tham Thanh Lan's legs, breathed in her sorrows, longed for forgiveness himself. He heard the yelping of a dog on the street, then nothing but Tham Thanh Lan's mournful pleasure. When she kissed him back, she bloodied his lips with her ardor, stole the breath from his lungs. Then she eased him inside her river of honey until they mingled their sweet distant waters.

A heavy shelf of clouds settled over Saigon as Tham Thanh Lan slept. The wind moaned a continual dank music, played an African *refrán* in Domingo's head: *The breeze is wind but the hurricane is also wind.*

On and off he slept, but mostly he watched Tham Thanh Lan. He was consoled by her steady breathing, by her smudged, unmoving lips. He traced a finger along her hipbone, touched the faint blue pulsing at her brow. She looked serene, a spray of fallen blossoms. Only her feet moved, as if they were hurrying somewhere, alternately twitching with dreams. For the first time since leaving Cuba, Domingo had no wish but to remain exactly where he was.

> *Dos gardenias para tí*
> *Con ellas quiero decir:*
> *Te quiero, te adoro, mi vida*
> *Ponle todo tu atención*
> *Porque son tu corazón y el mío . . .*

Domingo dreamed about the blind fishes of Cuba. He'd seen them in the sinkholes south of Alquízar, where he'd gone with his high school science club. The fishes' eyes had degenerated, and their skin was nearly transparent. They'd remained motionless, suspended near the walls and at the bottoms of the holes. In his dream, he'd swum with the fishes in their frigid sinkholes, round and round in the lightlessness until he grew fins on his belly and back.

Tham Thanh Lan stirred next to him, whispering something in Vietnamese. Domingo looked at her face and wondered what love had to do with memory. Did it ransack the past the way a song could? The body, he suspected, stored everything in its flesh. The sun-warmed spots of his childhood bed. The palms along Parque Martí postponing dusk. His Tío Eutemio had told him once that every person carried the scars of each year in his body like a thick-trunked tree.

Several people came to visit Tham Thanh Lan while she slept. Her boss from the Bamboo Den arrived, fingering a silver dinner bell, and threatened to dock her pay. When Domingo wouldn't open the door, the boss forced his way in and shook Tham Thanh Lan's shoulder, but he couldn't rouse her. He held his knobbly ear to her mouth, satisfied himself that she was breathing, and went off in a storm of obscenities.

Another bar girl, a mixed-blood friend of Tham Thanh Lan's, stopped by with dried plums. She stood by Tham Thanh Lan's bed, looking subdued and desultory, as if she'd been brought there for sale.

"I thought she was sick," she said. Her hands fluttered by her sides, trying to erase any lingering danger.

Domingo had heard the stories about the French families from Bordeaux and Nantes who'd come to Guantánamo to make their fortunes in sugar. What fortunes, he wondered, had the French searched for in Vietnam?

Domingo told her that Tham Thanh Lan wouldn't be returning to work. "I'll take care of her from now on." He was surprised at the resolve in his voice.

A pair of American soldiers knocked hard on the door an hour later. They checked the apartment number against their crumpled paper, sagged with disappointment when Domingo answered.

"How much longer?" the squat blond one asked.

"Never!" Domingo shouted back and slammed the door.

After three days, Tham Thanh Lan awoke. She didn't move at first but simply stared at the ceiling. Her hands sought the open plane of her belly, her wounded swell of moist silk. She caressed herself, stroking every welt and scar between her legs. Finally, she turned to Domingo and smiled: "I have a baby inside. I have a small world."

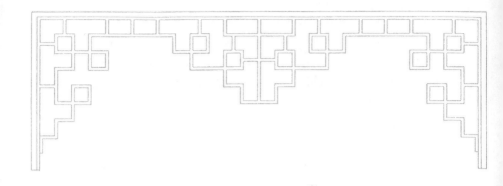

Peonies

HAVANA
(1899)

It was a Sunday morning in April, prematurely hot. Chen Pan didn't want to visit the Chinese cemetery, but Lucrecia had insisted. It was a holiday and people would be taking food and flowers to their ancestors. They would decorate their family's headstones with lanterns and red paper, too, report the year's happenings to the dead. The scent of burning incense would fill the air.

Chen Pan put on his white linen suit, the color of

mourning in China. He was sixty-two years old. Lucrecia was forty-eight. How could she be dying? The best doctors in Chinatown had confirmed it, so it must be true. Lucrecia was black inside her female parts, her womb withered to nothing. Overnight her hair had turned white. Now it was thin and straight as corn silk. Lucrecia had wanted to shave her head like a Chinese monk's, but Chen Pan had dissuaded her.

The doctors in Chinatown had tried every remedy—aloe root that had been dug up in winter, sugarcane exposed three years to frost, ardisia mingled with the curative herbs provided by trusted *santeros*. Nothing helped. Poor Lucrecia, they said, would be dead by July.

"What's taking you so long?" Lucrecia was dressed in her Easter outfit. Her hat was huge, festooned with blue ribbons and tulle. A feathered replica of a hummingbird was perched precariously on the rim. She looked younger today, as though possessed by a life-giving force. In a lacquered basket she carried candles for the dead. She'd wrapped the tapers in the thinnest of paper, a sunflower-green.

It seemed to Chen Pan that Lucrecia had worried excessively about pleasing their neighbors. Now she was seeking favor with her future ones, too. He slipped on his shoes, tying and retying the laces until they were symmetrical. He didn't want to deny Lucrecia anything these last months, but was this visit to the cemetery necessary?

Chen Pan had been up since before dawn. The rims of his eyes were red and swollen, as if he'd been drinking wine past midnight. Age and understanding were supposed to bring tranquility, but they'd brought him nothing of the sort. Last night, he'd had the same dream again: a hungry wolf followed him at a fixed distance, waiting to eat him. He had woken up so terrified that he couldn't fall back asleep. Today, he decided, he would choose the more peaceful alternative of an afternoon nap. The dream reminded him of the widow from the mountains who'd come to his village when he was a boy. People said she'd lost her mind after a wolf had snatched her infant son from her doorstep.

Lucrecia was waiting for Chen Pan downstairs, smoking a small cigar. Dr. Chu, who had long, flowing hair like Saint Liu, blamed the cigars for aggravating Lucrecia's condition. He said that women's bodies were not designed to properly absorb smoke, that it bypassed their lungs and was inhaled directly into their wombs, irreversibly poisoning them.

"You heard what the doctor said," Chen Pan reprimanded her. "Are you in such a hurry to leave me?"

"¡Por favor! If what he said was true, half of Havana would also be dying!"

It was no use arguing with Lucrecia. Once she'd

been a reasonable woman. Now she bickered with everyone, especially their daughter. Caridad had threatened to run away if they didn't let her join the traveling theater troupe from Camagüey. Soon, Chen Pan thought sadly, they would have to marry her off.

Some days the pain in Lucrecia's womb kept her in bed. Other days she seemed almost fine, and she and Chen Pan would walk along the shore to watch the frigate birds plunge into the sea. To him, Lucrecia's impending death felt like a voyage he was preparing to take to a foreign land—to China, perhaps, where he kept promising they'd go before she died.

"Come on, we don't have all day!" Lucrecia said. She took his arm as they walked down Calle Zanja.

The stores were closed, but a few vendors were roaming the street. One bedraggled man sold *garapina* from a giant jar on his head. Chen Pan bought two cups of the fermented pineapple drink. It was so sweet it made his molars ache. After forty-two years in Cuba, Chen Pan hadn't grown accustomed to the amount of sugar in everything. In China, white sugar was a luxury for the stoutly rich. Here it was so common that handfuls of the stuff were tossed into soups and stews.

Lucrecia drank her *garapina* with a long swallow. How could she be so sick, Chen Pan wondered, and still drink like that?

Yesterday she'd woken up in a sweat that had stuck

to his fingers like glue. And she'd been giving off a scent that he didn't recognize as hers—a combination of alcohol and old straw. Lucrecia must have noticed it, too, because she bathed night and day with an array of new soaps, bubbling and lathering like a spawning river crab.

"Esperanza Yu told me that Peking has the best opera. She said there's an acrobat there who can turn ninety-six somersaults in a row."

"We could go and be home in five months," Chen Pan offered.

"If you don't want to bury me in the Chinese cemetery, then bury me in the garden. This way, I'll help the vegetables grow."

How Lucrecia loved her garden! The fig tree with its stubborn roots. The rows of herbs lovingly arranged in brocades of green. The butterflies that browsed through her bougainvillea like customers at the Lucky Find. Who would take care of it all when she was gone? Only his great-aunt in China had loved her garden more. At night, the scent of her flowers had mingled with those of the wheat fields and river weeds.

"Before I die, I want to go to the mountains. You said yourself it's where the powers of heaven and earth meet."

"That's only true for China," Chen Pan said.

"I don't see why this can't be true for Cuba, too."

Lucrecia's family was from the Sierra Maestra, and from the Congo before that. Her grandparents had been runaway slaves, *cimarrones,* like Chen Pan. For years they'd lived in a cluster of *bohíos* in the mountains outside Guantánamo and had grown okra, corn, pumpkins, and sweet potatoes. Lucrecia had told him that her uncle had gotten so hungry once that he'd boiled his mother's cat for soup. This was the same uncle who'd later sold his sister to that bastard Don Joaquín in Havana.

O n Calle San Nicolás, a shoe seller idled by with his offerings suspended on a rod. *"¡Zapátos! ¡Zapatillas!"* Lucrecia stopped to inspect the slippers on display. She concentrated on picking out an attractive pair for her burial. Chen Pan sighed. How could she be so macabre? Didn't she care about his feelings at all?

Lucrecia selected a pair of embroidered high heels, but the vendor didn't carry her size. It was true that her feet were exceptionally large and she'd often had her shoes custom-made. For this the merchants in Chinatown had criticized her. Moss-tongued men who knew nothing of love, Chen Pan thought. To them, a man with a woman was commonplace, a need of the body, nothing more. They saved their deepest affections for each other.

When they'd suggested to Chen Pan that he go fetch a bride in China, like Ibrahim Wo had done, Chen Pan ignored them. Everyone had admired Ibrahim's wife, a fifteen year-old doll from C——, until she'd killed Ibrahim by poisoning his tea. Another child bride had committed suicide after setting eyes on her ancient groom. An unripe melon, Chen Pan had warned the men at the barbershop, didn't yield so easily to the knife.

His friends believed that women, by and large, were mankind's menace. How many kings and ministers, sages and saints, had been ruined by the presumably gentler sex? Recently, they'd heard reports from China that unfaithful wives no longer jumped in wells and that widows remarried without so much as threatening to commit suicide. "Such disrespect!" they cried. But Chen Pan didn't share their views.

He and Lucrecia had never married, but had this stopped their children from coming? Chen Pan had caressed Lucrecia's growing belly, teased her about being his concubine, claimed that there was no greater pleasure than bringing forth children late in life. "Too hot for cooking," he'd often announced, even in winter, and took her to eat at Oscar Shoy's noodle shop.

"*Mi amor,* I asked you a question." Lucrecia was looking at him with a puzzled expression.

"What is it?" Chen Pan turned toward her.

"After I die, will I become a ghost?" Lucrecia repeated.

Chen Pan didn't know how to answer her. While it was tempting to believe in the Pureland, he found it equally tempting to find peace in a blank and endless eternity.

"I'm not sure," Chen Pan said, and his spirits sank lower still.

On Calle Cuchillo, a bare-chested *mulato* sat on a mossy wall plucking the lice off his body and popping them into his mouth. Two men stumbled, drunk, out of a nearby gambling den. The smaller one was known for his powerful singing voice, and the other's face was as brown and creased as a walnut. Chen Pan also loved to gamble, but his family hadn't starved for this habit. His friends said that he was blessed with good fortune. This was true. His coins turned reliably to pesos, his pesos to silver, his silver to gold.

Lucrecia disapproved of Chen Pan's gambling, but she helped him with the riddles to the *charadas*. All of Havana was wild to play. Everyone talked about sheep and rats and peacocks until Chen Pan thought the whole city had gone mad. Last month, Lucrecia had correctly guessed the answer to this riddle: *One who is not a nun but always stays in her house.* The snail, of course.

Now their son, Desiderio, planned to open a gambling den four blocks from the Lucky Find. Lucrecia blamed Chen Pan for spoiling their oldest. Was this what happened when a man waited too long for a son? Chen Pan was convinced that there was too much heat in Desiderio's diet—fried pork and shredded beef washed down with multiple bottles of imported wine. Cooling foods would help him: fruit, vegetables, anything from the sea, crabs particularly. Or herbs like white peonies.

Fortunately, Lorenzo was more reasonable, gentle and deliberate and kind. How Chen Pan missed him! Why was it so impossible to keep a good son by his side? Ten years ago, Lorenzo had left for China and wrote to them every few months of his travels. Lucrecia believed that their son would come home before she died. Chen Pan said nothing to discourage her.

Down the street, Lucrecia stopped before a shop window filled with Spanish fans. Most ladies in Havana wouldn't go anywhere without one. How else could they say what they'd been taught never to directly express? Lucrecia was too plainspoken for such nonsense. In the center of the window, a hand-painted fan was displayed on a pedestal. Its sticks were made of ivory inlaid with gold, and tiny oval mirrors were mounted on the outer sides. Three hundred pesos at least, Chen Pan estimated. He hoped Lucrecia wasn't planning on including *that* in her grave.

A stolid matron in pleated satin rode by in her carriage, startling a beggar cooling himself off with a banana leaf. Chen Pan had seen the woman before—her round crimson face was unmistakable—but he couldn't remember precisely from where. Had she frequented his shop?

"There's one for you," Lucrecia joked, pointing to the matron's receding back. Lately, she'd begun encouraging him to look for another woman. This was more than Chen Pan could stand. There was no one he could ever love again and Lucrecia knew this.

"Bah!" Chen Pan snorted. He looked up at a row of royal palms against the flat, discolored sky. Everything was futile, he decided, equivalent to doing nothing at all. What was the point of working or talking, bathing or bargaining, when Lucrecia was dying?

If only the wine shops would open early, he'd stop and have a bowl or two. Maybe a plate of salted bamboo shoots to go with it. How else to endure this torment? When he was most mournful, Chen Pan drank his red wine and recited a poem.

> *Bathed in fragrance,*
> *do not brush your hat;*
> *Washed in perfume,*
> *do not shake your coat:*

Knowing the world
fears what is too pure,
The wisest man
prizes and stores light!

Mostly, the poems made Chen Pan lonely. And his loneliness was growing by the day, coiling about him like a snake. Long ago he'd dreamed of returning to his village, tall in his sedan chair, in the spring when the cassia trees were in bloom. That dream, like the others, had come to be forgotten, and Chen Pan had seen nothing in this to regret. So why were his old sadnesses coming now to flood and rot in his chest? He thought of his father, who'd been a hero for a few brief weeks after his death. Who besides Chen Pan would ever remember this?

It seemed to him that life's true tragedy was to lift up one's voice among the living and be met with indifference. In the barbershop the men spoke of the old ways, for which they had an inflated regard. They fondly recalled how criminals were expected to sing a line or two from an opera to entertain onlookers before their own beheadings. And warriors regularly carved out the hearts of their enemies, fried them in oil, and ate them to increase their courage.

But who, Chen Pan asked himself, was his enemy? Whose head could he knock against a wall? He knew only that he would've gladly eaten his share of hearts for a chance to save his wife.

Four years ago Chen Pan had wanted to saddle a horse and ride into battle behind José Martí. He'd wanted to fight this time, not just deliver a few weapons like he had during the Ten Years' War. Thirty years had passed, but what had it mattered to him that his hair and his eyebrows had grown white and his legs weak from city life? Somehow Lucrecia had managed to convince him to stay home.

Instead Chen Pan had ended up sending the rebels all the money he'd made off the Spaniards, who had departed Cuba by the shipload. Many of them had lost fortunes in the war and had disposed of their treasures in his shop. Quickly, Chen Pan had resold their things to his foreign clients at a high profit. He'd kept only one item—a rare hardwood cane carved into a snake that he'd bought from an old *gallego*.

It hadn't been easy to find food during the war, no matter how much money he made. Desperate neighbors had raided Lucrecia's garden, leaving them with nothing but taro weeds and sweet potato shoots to eat. The hard times had reminded Chen Pan of when he was a boy—the taxes and famines, the soldiers and bandits all squeezing his family dry.

He and Lucrecia had been at El Moro when the soldiers raised the Cuban flag. Thousands of people danced in the streets. Chen Pan, though, was in no mood to celebrate. He recalled how after the Civil War, Confederate refugees had come to Cuba from the American South and pawned their weapons and pearl stickpins at his shop. The Cubans had sat in the laps of those Americans like yapping little dogs, begging for scraps. Now they were disgracing themselves in a similar manner.

Several families were at the Chinese cemetery already, paying their respects to the dead. When Chen Pan had accompanied Lucrecia to the Colón cemetery last week, she hadn't liked it much. Most of the Cuban graves were not kept up. There were cobwebs everywhere and not nearly enough shade. Striped mosquitoes hummed amid the puddles and in damp pockets of soil.

In contrast, the Chinese cemetery looked as neat as Lucrecia's own kitchen. Willow trees were putting forth new shoots. The grass was moist and green. Nobody, it seemed, was forgotten. The graves of the gamblers and beggars and those with no family (including the hunchback who'd sold notions and spent all his free time in the teashop) were respectfully sprinkled with water, too. Here, no spirits went hungry.

Chen Pan and Lucrecia strolled along the cemetery's swept dirt paths, greeting the families picnicking beside the headstones. Hilario Eng and his brothers, all bean curd dealers, were solemnly gathered by their father's grave, setting out dishes and a bowl of warm rice. Others burned paper money or laid down their wreaths, and wailed.

For the New Year's sacrifice back home, the women used to kill chickens and geese and buy plenty of pork. They lined up along the river, washing rice for the festivities. Even Chen Pan's own mother, renowned for her indolence, joined in the scouring and scrubbing until her arms had turned red in the water. For days, the sounds of exploding firecrackers would sing in Chen Pan's head.

"That's it," Lucrecia said, smiling, indicating a shady spot under the pomegranate tree. "That's where I want to be buried."

Chen Pan tried to imagine his wife lying peacefully in a coffin, her hands nested at her waist just so. How could he ever bear to have the lid closed down upon her?

There was a crow perched on an upper branch of the pomegranate tree. *Send me a sign,* Chen Pan prayed, rubbing the medallion he kept in his pocket as a talisman. *Show me that Lucrecia won't die.* But the crow stood stiffly, as immobile as any statue in the Lucky Find. Chen Pan had made desperate pledges to his ancestors and to the Buddha and to Lucrecia's panoply of saints. What difference had it made?

When he'd returned from delivering his machetes to Commander Sian in 1869, Chen Pan had been prepared to die. It was Lucrecia who saved him. She bathed him, cleaning out a festering wound that kept him limping to this day. "You're lucky you don't have to cut off your leg altogether," she scolded.

Over the years, Chen Pan had revealed to her bits and pieces of that journey—of the camps overcrowded with dying men, of the cowardice of the Spaniards who'd left their wounded to rot in the battlefields. In the wildest parts of the mountains, the rebels had eaten sour oranges and the pulpy tops of palm trees. Sometimes they caught fat *jutías* and roasted them over fires. (In those days, the woods were so dense that the rodents could run in the treetops for weeks.)

Lucrecia had asked Chen Pan if he'd seen anyone killed. He told her about the Spanish soldier, a boy, really, who pleaded for his life in perfect Cantonese. This had shaken Commander Sian, but he slit the Spaniard's throat just the same.

Unhappy as he'd been, Lucrecia helped Chen Pan settle back on Calle Zanja. She painted their apartment a soothing blue and kept the Buddha's altar smoking with incense. Next to it she put a statue of Yemayá, in honor of her mother, and offered her watermelons and cane syrup, now and then a fresh hen. Chen Pan began wearing traditional Chinese clothes again, baggy cotton pants and wide-sleeved shirts.

None of his old dandy wardrobe. He decided that he wanted nothing more to do with anything modern.

If Lucrecia wanted to be buried under the pomegranate tree, Chen Pan sighed, he would arrange it. His best friend, Arturo Fu Fon, had told Chen Pan this: *Hope cannot be said to exist, nor can it be said not to exist. It is just like roads across the earth. For actually the earth had no roads to begin with, but when many men pass one way, a road is made.* Nobody ever knew whom Arturo Fu Fon was quoting, but it frequently sounded worthy of bamboo tablets and silk. For just such pronouncements—more than for his barely adequate haircuts and shaves—the men of Chinatown went to his barbershop.

In the far corner of the cemetery, a plump *chino* Chen Pan didn't recognize sat smoking a three-foot-long pipe with a pewter bowl. Chen Pan thought he might buy it for his shop. Would fifty pesos be enough? All manner of Chinese curios were becoming popular with the tourists from Europe. When his friends returned to China, he gave them money to pick up heirlooms for the Lucky Find. He easily made ten times his investment, sometimes much more than that.

Chen Pan bowed slightly and backed away, a disconcerting buzzing in his ears. He felt a cold wind blow into him, although the day was humid and the sky a sober blue. Around him the trees were still. A faint steam rose from the heavily watered graves. He had a sudden urge for watermelon, the jade-green ones that used to grow by the shore in China.

He rejoined Lucrecia under the pomegranate tree. She was deciding on the flowers that she wanted surrounding her grave. Recently, she had planted a bed of peonies for him in their garden. They were one of his favorite flowers and had grown wild in the fields outside his village. After Lucrecia was gone, he would gaze at the peonies, call her name in the breeze. Then he'd light a candle in her name and watch the smoke rise to heaven.

"Look at me." Lucrecia grabbed his sleeve.

Chen Pan said nothing. He felt as if his whole body were scattering like particles of dust. He imagined himself swirling higher and higher, merging with the passing clouds, inducing a lightning storm.

Lucrecia stared at him a long time. "More than half my life has been happy," she said softly. "How many people can say that?"

On the way home, Lucrecia had a sudden craving for shrimp in garlic sauce. Chen Pan took her to Alejandro Poey's restaurant on Calle Salud. She ordered dish after savory dish as

Chen Pan watched, too dispirited to eat anything himself.

When he was a boy, he'd spent days by the river digging up worms to fasten onto his homemade copper hooks. He and his friends had considered shrimp to be the most hopeless of creatures because they used their own pincers to push the point of the hooks into their mouths. Why, the stupidest fish had more sense than that!

After lunch Lucrecia's movements seemed slow and laborious, as though she were struggling underwater. She had difficulty climbing the steps to their apartment over the Lucky Find. By the time Chen Pan helped her reach the top, she was breathless and blaming it on the garlic sauce.

Painstakingly, Lucrecia removed her Easter hat and little jacket, her lavender bodice and layered skirts down to her petticoats. Then she sat on the edge of her bed and loosened her hair. Chen Pan pulled off her boots and stockings. Her feet were swollen and studded with blisters.

He brought her a handkerchief he'd rinsed in cool water and pressed it to her temples. Lucrecia's eyes seemed unusually large, the whites clean as starched napkins. She looked so flushed and beautiful that Chen Pan almost kissed her on the mouth. Instead he settled her to sleep and held her hand. Lucrecia's wrist pulsed rapidly, like something apart from her, a captured bird, its brown plumage smooth and dry. Suddenly, it lay still.

Outside, the dark, lowering clouds flashed with lightning and the temperature dropped sharply. If this weren't Cuba, Chen Pan might have expected it to snow, big plum-blossom petals of snow that would flutter to earth and thickly mute, for the afternoon, all signs of life.

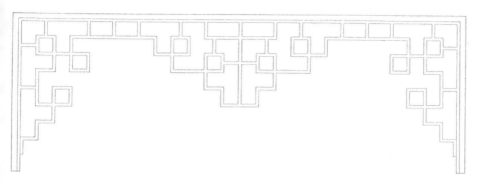

The Little War

SANTIAGO TO HAVANA
(1912)

Chen Pan was sitting in a barber's chair in Santiago de Cuba when Lorenzo, Chen Pan's son, received the news that his wife had gone into labor early with their third child. Lorenzo's hair was only half cut as he bolted from under Francisco Ting's scissors. It was a seventeen-hour journey by train back to Havana under the best of circumstances, and the times were not good. Yesterday word had spread that *los negros* were rising up, arming themselves

183

with muskets and machetes, readying to launch a bloody race war that would leave every criollo dead.

Chen Pan didn't believe this was true. But what did his opinion matter? He saw how the *chinos* were treated, even the respected ones like Lorenzo. When the criollos needed medical attention, they were very solicitous of his expertise—it was Doctor Chen this and Doctor Chen that. In fact, the mayor of Santiago, Perequito Pérez, had thrown a banquet in Lorenzo's honor after Lorenzo had cured him of a debilitating leg spasm. But Chen Pan was immune to their flattering tongues. When the times grew difficult or the jobs scarce, he knew well enough that they were just *chinos de porquería.*

The train station was crowded with people battling to get on the afternoon train to Havana. Chen Pan leaned against the ticket booth as he watched Lorenzo maneuver his way around the station. With one hand, Lorenzo held on to his son Meng, with the other, he grasped his satchel of herbs and curing potions. Their suitcases were back at Fong's hotel, the bill unpaid. There would be time enough to rectify this once they were home.

Lorenzo returned with three first-class seats. Chen Pan wasn't surprised. His son had survived for more than a decade in China barely knowing the language. Chen Pan laughed when Lorenzo told him how he'd exchanged six months' worth of potency powder for the tickets. It turned out the stationmaster was an habitué of the dance halls of Santiago, and his troubles had come, conveniently, to Lorenzo's attention as he'd made his rounds last week. Chen Pan, Lorenzo, and Meng pushed their way to their compartment and settled in the empty seats by the window.

A stiff-looking couple sat down next to them. The woman wore an elaborate wide-brimmed hat and a gold lorgnette. They were Belgian, they said, and had just come from visiting their daughter and Cuban son-in-law in San Luís. The experience had displeased them immensely. The other passenger, a femininely elegant young man in buttoned vest and polished boots, spent most of his time posing in the mirror above his seat. His boots squeaked each time he shifted his feet.

The steam engine billowed and roared. On the platform, the vendors were making their last sales. Lorenzo bought half a dozen ham sandwiches and a large bottle of mandarin juice. Meng ate eagerly. He was only seven, but he was as tall and corpulent as a ten-year-old. His older brother, Shoy, was thinner and looked many years Meng's junior. Chen Pan wondered what his third grandson—he never doubted it would be a boy—would look like. He'd suggested naming him Pipo, like the happy chiming of a bird.

If only Lucrecia had lived long enough to see their grandchildren! It seemed impossible that she'd been dead thirteen years. Chen Pan recalled how she'd given birth to their own children, expelling them like damp red blossoms with hardly any trouble at all. Lucrecia had been buried in the Chinese cemetery in the shade of the pomegranate tree, just as she'd wanted. Chen Pan's plot was waiting next to hers. Often he adjusted the time in his mind so that Lucrecia was still with him, living in his flesh, her hair a springy black. He unfolded his memories of her delicately, turning them this way and that. What else was there for him to do?

Chen Pan hadn't been so old when Lucrecia had died. His friends had told him that he should take another wife, father more children. They'd looked up to him then. "There goes Chen Pan," they'd said. "He lived in the forest for a year, then opened the biggest store in Chinatown." The elderly criollas had continued to flirt with him in his shop. "Ay, Señor Chen, you are the lucky find here!" they'd crooned, tottering back to their carriages.

Now here was Lorenzo awaiting the birth of another son. Lorenzo had met his second wife at her buckwheat noodle stall in Canton. Chen Pan understood why his son had fallen in love with Jinying. It was obvious that she had excellent *ch'i*. Her blood sang with energy and her eyes were bright with life, everything in balance. Her cooking was a perfect blend of elements, too.

Lorenzo had three more children back in China with his first wife, two girls and a boy. If Lucrecia had been alive, she would have made the journey to visit them. Lorenzo said that his first wife was beautiful, but like the stars she was coldly inhospitable. He sent her money so their children would lack nothing— ample dowries for the girls; a scholar's education for the boy. Perhaps one day the boy would come to Cuba and teach them all Chinese.

Dusk lingered on the horizon, giving the mountains a preternatural glow, as though someone had set a fire deep inside them. There was a commotion in the corridor. Chen Pan saw two men come to blows over the contradictory reports in the newspapers. The fat one shouted that a posse of *negros* had raped a schoolteacher in Ramón de las Yaguas and had partially cannibalized her flesh. Was he unsteady on his feet from the lurching train or from too much drink? His wiry scrap of an opponent took offense at the fat man's remarks and slapped him in the face.

Chen Pan felt as if two stones were pressed against his temples. How was it that fear so clotted rational thinking? He was forty years older than these fools, but he could think far more clearly. Chen Pan gestured toward the men and gave his son a look of disgust. Lorenzo shrugged. What was there to do? Already Meng was snoring gently, his cheek flattened by the windowpane. The Belgians remained unperturbed, their eyes glued to their leather-bound books.

Chen Pan noticed a garland of geese flying resolutely south. A tumbledown shack sat neglected at the edge of a sugarcane field. If the arguing men didn't look too closely, they might take his son for a light-skinned *mulato*. At second glance, they would see that Lorenzo's eyes were 100 percent Chinese. Would they lynch him to be safe? Chen Pan knew that every man, in his way, was particularly plagued—beset by northern winds, rotting with winter dampness, boiling with summer heat. What did any of it have to do with race?

Smoke from a nearby fire obscured the view to the north. Could they be clearing the sugarcane fields this early in the year? The train pulled into the station at Jiguaní, which was thick with the foul black smoke. Boys with handkerchiefs over their faces were selling late-edition newspapers. Chen Pan caught sight of a headline: NEGROS ON A RAMPAGE IN ORIENTE! Just then their compartment door swung open, and the steward, gaunt in his crisp white uniform, began serving them cookies and tea from a rolling cart. The Belgian couple laid down their books and partook of the offerings.

"Baba!" Meng woke up and started to cry. He

pointed out the window. By the tracks lay two corpses, shot in the head, their brains uncoiling in the dirt.

Judging from their clothes, Chen Pan guessed they were rural laborers, farmhands or cane cutters. Others on the train saw the dead men, too, because all at once an uproar ensued, louder than the engine itself as it pulled out of the station. One thick-legged woman in a polka-dot dress ran down the corridor screaming that *los negros* had commandeered the train. Her hands were shaking and she looked as though she might faint.

Lorenzo held Meng in his lap. The boy was sucking his middle finger. Lorenzo gave him a pinch of kaolin powder to take with his juice. Chen Pan wanted to comfort his grandson, to smooth his hair and make the dead men go away. But another part of him wanted to force Meng to look at them again and learn that evil existed in every hour. Lorenzo rocked his son as the train picked up speed. Over their shoulders, three hanged men swung from the limbs of a coral tree. The high-pitched twittering of the warblers cut the air in a thousand places.

Chen Pan adjusted his legs to a more comfortable position and unwrapped a ham sandwich. The Belgian couple and the Cuban dandy had fallen asleep. From his satchel Lorenzo removed a copy of the *Yellow Emperor's Classics of Internal Medicine,* which he was translating from Chinese to Spanish. Lorenzo had grown bored with this effort, preferring to focus on his own anecdotal history of Chinese herbs.

"You've grown old from too much work," Chen Pan chided him.

"And you're still a hardy goat." Lorenzo was bemused. "Not so much as a trace of gout."

"You've spoken the truth." Chen Pan grinned. "And these teeth are all mine, original condition."

"Regular antiques. You could sell them in your shop," Lorenzo laughed.

"Only I'm hard of hearing on my left side."

"So turn your head to the right."

"*Sí,* Doctor."

Chen Pan looked out the window at the passing sugarcane fields, at their endless, swaying green. How inviting they looked from this distance. Who could fathom the mountain of corpses that had made these fields possible? If he had one fantasy left, it was this: to purchase La Amada plantation, sign his name to the deed. He was well off and his credit was good. He might have succeeded with the help of a few fellow merchants. But his aversion to sugarcane was deeper than any sense of vengeance.

"Sometimes I make myself tired," Chen Pan sighed. "Perhaps it's time I was dead."

"Nonsense, Papá."

"Did you hear that?" Chen Pan asked suddenly, tilting his head. It was a disagreeable sound, a muted hooting, as if an owl were trapped among the luggage racks. But Lorenzo had buried himself in his book. Chen Pan would have liked to converse more. It was good for his spirits, but he knew his son wasn't much of a talker.

So much had happened during the twelve years that Lorenzo had wandered through China. Lucrecia had died. Cuba had won its freedom from Spain. Desiderio had opened his gambling den and become the father of twins. Even Caridad had settled down after a quixotic singing career and finally married a quiet shopkeeper in Viñales.

Lorenzo had journeyed to Chen Pan's village by sedan chair and spice-wood boat. The children there had been barefoot, their heads full of lice, their bellies swollen with hunger and worms (no different from these parts). Chen Pan's younger brother had been weakly tending what remained of the family's wheat farm. Lorenzo had treated his uncle with numerous kidney remedies, all fruitlessly. (The more remedies prescribed for a disease, Lorenzo contended, the less likely it was to be cured.) Chen Pan wondered when it would be his turn to die.

His son had returned to Havana a stranger after being a foreigner abroad. Now where could he call home? Lorenzo's skin, Chen Pan supposed, was a home of sorts, with its accommodations to three continents. Or perhaps home was in the blood of his grandsons as it traveled through their flesh.

Recently, Chen Pan had taken to closing the Lucky Find for weeks at a time and accompanying Lorenzo on his doctoring rounds throughout Cuba. After so many years without his son, he couldn't bear to be apart from him for long. Last fall, they'd gone to Remedios and had seen Chinese puppeteers in the street. With much fanfare, the performers had burned a flurry of papers, then poked through the ashes with ordinary sticks to retrieve colored ribbons. Lucrecia's life had been like that, Chen Pan thought, stolen from the ashes, then burst open with carnival reds.

It was after midnight. Through the window, the hills looked artificial with their dark fixed palms. The lights of another town were coming into view, flaring like a multitude of candles. The train approached Victoria de las Tunas and would soon arrive in Camagüey. Lorenzo and Meng were asleep, breathing in unison.

If only their locomotive could fly, they'd be back in Havana in no time. Chen Pan had seen pictures of the new American and French planes, fragile-looking contraptions with dragonfly wings. He grew drowsy imagining the train slowly ascending, overtaking the clouds, outrunning the thunder from the east. Then he dreamed that each car was a child's coffin festooned with boughs of jasmine, one little coffin after another strung together like the tail of a high-flying kite, a parade of shiny coffins flying toward the sun.

Chen Pan awoke with a start in the middle of the night. Sleep was such a nuisance. He'd just as soon do away with it altogether than endure these maddening interruptions. He slept very little, three or four fitful hours at most. Yesterday, at least, it had come in handy. At five in the morning, he'd woken up in his hotel room in Santiago just in time to find a tarantula on his chest.

Before dawn, Meng woke up calling for his mother. Chen Pan reached for his grandson and patted his sticky fingers. *"Aquí estoy, gordito."* The lights from a passing station stuttered over the boy's face. Chen Pan offered him the bottle of mandarin juice and Meng drank, dribbling some down the front of his shirt.

"I want to tell you something important," Chen Pan whispered. "In your life there will be two paths, one easy and one difficult. Listen well: Always choose the difficult one."

Chen Pan wanted to explain to Meng that *los negros* were protesting for their right to form a political party, that they would pay for their protesting with their lives and the lives of many innocent others.

What choice did they have? Revolutions never took place sitting quietly under a mango tree. Men grew tired of tolerating misery, of waiting for better days.

"Who's taking care of Jade Peach?" Meng demanded.

"I don't know," Chen Pan said.

Lorenzo yawned. "Go back to sleep, *hijo.*"

But Meng was wide awake. At home he was in charge of feeding the family parrot, an extraordinary bird. Jade Peach ate from a spoon, greeted visitors in Spanish and Chinese, and imitated the broadcasters on the radio. Occasionally, she gave Lorenzo's patients her own diagnoses: *This is a difficult case, Señora.* Or: *Take this lime powder three times a day, and you'll feel better soon.*

"Your brother is watching her," Lorenzo murmured.

"She'll die!" Meng whined.

Chen Pan knew that Meng was right. His older brother would most likely forget to replenish the water and seed. Meng sullenly pulled a thread on his sleeve, partly unraveling the cuff. Then he yawned so wide his pink throat was visible.

"When will we get there?"

"By lunchtime," Lorenzo said. "Now go back to sleep."

Behind the morning clouds, the sun hesitantly stirred. The Cuban dandy was talking in his sleep. Chen Pan couldn't make out his mumbling except for the phrase "these damn centipedes," which he angrily repeated. The Belgians were also asleep. Chen Pan studied their faces and wondered if they'd ever been in love, stayed up whole nights in restless passion.

Before Lucrecia had gotten sick, they'd often made love twice a day—early in the morning before the children woke up and again at night, after they went to bed. Chen Pan would have preferred spending more time romancing his wife's body, but she hadn't encouraged his lingering. Sometimes when they'd slowed down enough, he'd felt Lucrecia's pleasure ringing from her body to his.

Since her death he hadn't so much as visited a brothel. How could he have betrayed her? Besides, Lorenzo reported that the whorehouses had gotten dangerous in recent years. He spoke of their ruinous effects on his clients: carbuncled testicles, penile lesions, pustules, and malodorous discharges that took an arsenal of ointments to treat. Certainly, Chen Pan had heard enough to keep his own temptations in check.

Still, he fantasized about bedding one last woman— a true tigress, someone who would dance for him in the scantiest of silks, make love to him for hours, collapse with him in happy, erotic exhaustion. But how could he face Lucrecia on the other side after an escapade like that?

For Chen Pan's seventieth birthday, Benito Sook

had sent him a saucy whore recently arrived from Hong Kong. A moth-browed girl, she had flawless skin and a plum-ripe mouth. She looked like that Fire Swan, the trapeze artist from Amoy long ago. But the Hong Kong girl's eyes were ruined, Chen Pan noticed, raw as two wounds. He shooed her away with a fistful of bills so she would reveal nothing of what hadn't transpired.

The train approached the Santa Clara station, its paint badly blistered from the sun. Chen Pan had been to the station earlier in the year. It was here that he and Lorenzo had changed trains for the Cienfuegos Line to visit Lorenzo's patients in Santa Isabel de las Lajas, Cruces, and Cienfuegos. In the opposite direction was Sagua la Grande, with its lively Chinatown. It was Chen Pan's favorite city after Havana.

In a distant field, Chen Pan spotted a dozen men chained together and marching at gunpoint. They were bareheaded, in rags, without the machetes they would normally be carrying. For what abominations had they been blamed? More to the point, how many of them would be alive by week's end? Chen Pan wanted to wake up his grandson and tell him something more: *Few things are as certain as hatred, mi amor.*

The Belgian couple woke up to the early morning chaos of the station. Soon the steward came by, offering them a breakfast of sweet rolls and coffee. Meng ate voraciously, smearing his bread with all the butter on his plate. Lorenzo wasn't hungry. He complained that his back was sore from sleeping all night on the torturous seats. Chen Pan accompanied his grandson to the rest room. They squeezed past the passengers in the corridor, glimpsing others behind the thick partitions of glass. He was astonished at the endless layers of crinoline the criollas wore in the dead heat of summer.

In the toilet, Chen Pan noticed that Meng's penis was practically the size of a man's. Chen Pan hoped that the boy would grow into it. Overly large *pingas* were as problematic as too small ones, he'd learned from the seductive Delmira years ago. She'd complained about a certain *guajiro* who'd been built like a lead pipe and had damaged her inside. Later, Delmira had announced with no small satisfaction that the man had died from an equine disease he'd gotten while copulating with a mare.

A new passenger was in their compartment when Chen Pan and his grandson returned. The man introduced himself as Rodolfo Cañizares and said he was on his way to Havana to assume a post with the Ministry of the Interior. His jaw was clean-shaven and strikingly capacious, the size of a small pumpkin.

He was talking to the Belgians in a painfully loud Spanish.

"How are things in Paris? Do you still eat snails there?" He pulled some snuff from a leather pouch and offered it all around.

The Belgians stared at him blankly. Chen Pan laughed in spite of his instant distaste for the stranger. His oiled hair and studied manner reminded Chen Pan of his eldest son. Desiderio was a year older than Lorenzo and despised everything Chinese. It grieved Chen Pan that his own son was ashamed of him, of his accent and the Chinese "pajamas" he wore. On Christmas Day, Desiderio sent a creaky *quitrín* to pick him up at the Lucky Find. For one strictly supervised hour, Chen Pan got to visit his other grandchildren.

Chen Pan opened the window and let the wind blow against his face. The Zapata Swamp claimed a shoe-shaped peninsula of saw grass and cow-lily leaves to the south. Lorenzo was convinced that he could find herbs there for his curing potions. It had become impossible for him to obtain ingredients from China. Last summer, he'd contacted two herbal importers in San Francisco, but their products had proved inferior.

The number of Lorenzo's clients was dwindling. Few Chinese were immigrating to Cuba, preferring instead to go to the United States. Chen Pan knew that most of the old former coolies, like himself, had died or gone back home for good. These days, there were more funerals than births in Chinatown. The younger generations hardly considered themselves Chinese. And they preferred more modern medical methods, too, demanding overnight results even if it ended up killing them.

The land of Matanzas province was unremarkable and flat. Here and there, Chen Pan spotted a cluster of *bohíos* or a dilapidated general store (invariably run by an irascible *gallego*). Only an occasional flushing poinciana enlivened the view. In China, so many people believed that Cuba was a land of lush jungles that Lorenzo said he'd ended up believing it himself. Upon his return, he'd had to reacquaint himself with the island, with its lusterless plains and dull acres of sugarcane. Sometimes Chen Pan forgot that the sea was never more than thirty miles away.

Meng looked quietly out the window. It seemed to Chen Pan that his grandson was happiest in silence, that the very sound of words caused him discomfort. Why, the boy hadn't uttered a word until he was three. His older brother had spoken for him. *Little Brother wants more rice.* Or *Meng says there are thirty-two sparrows in the laurel tree.* What Meng finally said when he'd opened his mouth was: "I want pistachio ice cream with extra chocolate sauce."

Lorenzo feared that his son was unintelligent, but Chen Pan insisted that this wasn't true. Little Meng, he said, was a born mathematician, multiplying and dividing long before he attended school. He'd proved adept with Chen Pan's abacus and frequently helped Lorenzo barter his services. When a patient had no money to pay him, it was Meng who suggested that a tin of kerosene might do instead.

Chen Pan couldn't get used to his son's way of doing business. On any given day Lorenzo might receive as payment chickens, guava paste, tallow candles, salt cod, rum, hatchets, hammocks, yams, or a basket of freshly caught crabs. Four years ago, Lorenzo had gotten Jade Peach after eliminating a baseball-size goiter on a shipwright's neck.

It wasn't easy being *el médico chino.* Everywhere Lorenzo turned, he saw disease and debility. Chen Pan, too, had learned to detect the sickness in people's eyes, in the texture of their skin and their faltering movements. On a stroll through the plaza or in a passing donkey cart, he spotted diabetes, hepatitis, cancers, tumors, so many failing hearts.

And, of course, there were the people whom his son's herbs and ointments couldn't cure. The notary in Cárdenas who wore a fur coat every day of the summer. Or the blue-eyed laundress who fancied herself the Queen of the Geese and ate grain from a gilded dish. What medicaments did he have for them?

Near Güines, a wedding procession snaked along a dirt road toward a whitewashed church. The horses were bedecked with a profusion of ribbons, and Chen Pan imagined that he could hear the jingling of their harness bells. At the end of the line was the bride's carriage, entwined with a thousand camellias. Chen Pan's heart rose an inch, swelling with good wishes for the unseen couple. How young they would probably seem to him, how naïve.

The Cuban dandy awoke with a gargling sound and examined Cañizares sideways, like a bird of prey. He began his morning ablutions, which included anointing every exposed inch of his skin with gardenia oil. Then he excavated a bag of walnuts from his suitcase and began cracking them so loudly it sounded like pistol shots. The noise alarmed the occupants of the neighboring compartments, who began shouting again that the train was under siege.

The downpour came from nowhere. One moment the sky was as blue and enameled as French china and the next, a herd of clouds raced across it, goaded by the wind. The birds flew about in a frenzy, seeking dry places to wait out the rain. A sapodilla tree shivered, lamenting its still-unripe fruit. Tiny bud, kernel of boy awaiting them in Havana! In just a few hours more, Chen Pan thought, the train would arrive and he would meet his new grandson.

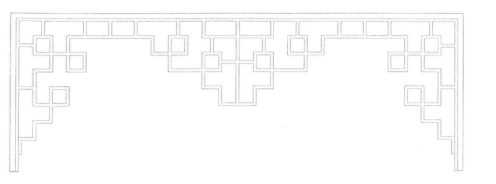

Incense

For the first few months of her pregnancy, Tham Thanh Lan ate only bitter foods. Pickled melons. Quail eggs in salted vinegar. Dirt-encrusted roots she collected on the outskirts of town and boiled to make soups. She spread fish sauce on everything, including the Neapolitan ice cream Domingo brought her from the PX. He offered her American treats— peanut butter and saltines, Oreo cookies, hamburger meat. But all these foods nauseated her.

Now Tham Thanh Lan kissed Domingo only if he smeared *nước mắm* on his lips first. To make love, he had to spread the fish sauce everywhere.

Domingo tried to teach Tham Thanh Lan Spanish, another language of the body. *Mi reina. Mi adoración. Eres mi sueño.* She said that they were having a boy and Domingo didn't doubt her. He taught her how to say *mi hijo,* my son. But she wasn't interested in learning new words.

He wanted to show Tham Thanh Lan how to dance, but her hips resisted.

"I'm too tired," she said, and settled down for another nap.

Domingo went on a shopping spree, bought Tham Thanh Lan things she didn't need: hair curlers and a waffle iron, lemon cake mix, and a brand-new sewing machine that she sold for a fortune to a tailor who fitted uniforms for the Vietnamese navy. He bought Tham Thanh Lan a radio, but she made him return it.

"No more sound," she insisted. Even turned down to a crackle, music made her unbearably sad.

Domingo couldn't get used to the silence, to the monotony of her sleeping. Soon he was hearing music everywhere—in the ping and hiss of the new teapot; in the percussive rumble of his stomach. *Tintintintin patá patí.* Who was he without a little rhythm?

His Tío Eutemio had told him that during slavery days, drumming had been forbidden altogether. The sugar mill owners hadn't wanted their "property" getting overly excited and sending messages to slaves on other plantations. In those times, to own a drum, to play a drum, were acts of rebellion punishable by death. And so the drums and the drummers learned to whisper instead.

The day Domingo brought Tham Thanh Lan an electric fan, she told him that he would leave her, ride horses in a place with blazing rocks and no trees, a landscape Domingo had trouble imagining. Then she turned on the fan and lay down in front of the artificial breeze. Behind her, the sticky curtains stirred.

She dreamed of crabs, dead and rotting on riverbanks, their casings picked clean by seagulls and sand fleas. Tham Thanh Lan recalled the summer the Mekong River died, how the fishermen's nets pulled only dead fish from its depths. Sometimes she woke up frightened, thinking a crab had replaced the baby in her womb. "It moved like a crab! It ran sideways!" she cried until Domingo soothed her with fish sauce kisses, placed his hands on her belly, and said, "*Mi amor,* crabs don't kick like that."

His mother had blamed the *yanquis* for every deformed baby she'd delivered in Guantánamo—the infant born with an eye in his umbilicus; the hairdresser's triplets attached like paper dolls by their hands and feet. The Americans, she said, had dumped poisons into the Río Guaso, contaminating the sugarcane fields, making the coffee trees redden with blight. One Easter Mamá had delivered a Haitian boy whose heart had steamed furiously outside his chest. A moment later, his tiny heart had exploded in her face like a grenade.

Domingo took Tham Thanh Lan for walks in the flame tree garden behind the Buddhist temple. He entertained her with stories about the general he drove around all day. General Arnold F. Bishop had an artificial leg that replaced the one he'd lost in Korea. The leg kept coming loose at inopportune moments. Last week they'd hit a bump on a country road and his leg flew out of the jeep, knocking a startled peasant off his water buffalo.

In March, Domingo was away for ten days driving the general in an armored convoy to inspect the troops in the South. General Bishop was a big Bob Hope fan and looked forward to the Christmas shows every year. He claimed he'd fucked one of those Gold Digger showgirls, a kinky one from Kansas City who'd gotten off sucking the stump of his leg. "Damn, it gives you something to kill for!" General Bishop exclaimed.

Domingo had seen the Christmas show his first winter in Vietnam. The women were skinny and flat-assed, no breasts to speak of, their legs all horse-bone and sinew. Plus he didn't get the jokes. Not a single one. He missed the girls of Guantánamo—their stretch shorts and the tight-fitting military uniforms that showed off every curve. The year he left, they were wearing a Polish perfume that smelled like a mixture of wisteria and gasoline.

What would General Bishop know about any of this? Still, when the general offered Domingo his regular girl in My Tho, he didn't refuse.

When he returned to Saigon, Tham Thanh Lan had barely eaten or slept. Her dark, swollen eyes accused him. How had she known that he'd slept with another woman?

"You'll marry me, right?" Tham Thanh Lan demanded each time they made love. Domingo was always weak and grateful then. And always he said yes.

He knew from experience that pregnant women didn't act normally. He'd seen the butcher's wife, Leoncia Agudín, a religious woman, assault her husband with sailor-mouthed insults in Parque Martí. His crime: buying a *cucurucho* from the comely peanut vendor. Of course, she was five months' pregnant at the time. Women who had baby after baby were nicknamed *barrigonas* (there were many *barrigonas* in Guantánamo) and forgiven for a different standard of behavior altogether.

Domingo had grown up around these crazy pregnant women. They'd sat in his mother's kitchen, splashing rum into their morning coffee, hunched together over the latest scandal, laughing raucously over men, whom they'd ridiculed or lamented with such ferocity that it made Domingo ashamed to be a boy. His mother would see him blushing and say, "Don't worry, *mi cielo*. This has nothing to do with you."

The women had played Radio Mil Diez at top volume and danced with each other, colossal belly to belly, or pulled Domingo close and taught him how to cha-cha-chá. "*Así*, little Papi. Don't grind too much or the nice girls will refuse to dance with you." In this manner, he'd learned the secrets of women.

Domingo heard of GIs taking their Vietnamese fiancées or wives home after their tour of duty. The army frowned upon this, did everything possible to keep the couples apart, more so if children were involved. A few men had killed themselves for the love of these whores. Everyone said they'd been *gook hoodooed*. No cure for it except death itself.

Stories drifted back to Vietnam of former bar girls waking up in Georgia, bleaching their hair, wearing blue jeans and cowboy hats, renaming themselves Delilah. Other stories were sadder still. Of underaged girls dressed up like China dolls at their husbands' insistence, paraded around small towns in Texas or Mississippi, shopping for trinkets at Woolworth's. Saddest of all were the suicides—the poisonings, the slit wrists. Anything to set their souls free to fly home.

Domingo wondered about these migrations, these cross-cultural lusts. Were people meant to travel such distances? Mix with others so different from themselves? His great-grandfather had left China more than a hundred years ago, penniless and alone. Then he'd fallen in love with a slave girl and created a whole new race—brown children with Chinese eyes who spoke Spanish and a smattering of Abakuá. His first family never saw him again.

Domingo was permitted into the officers' club because he worked for General Bishop, but he wasn't welcomed there. His skin was too dark, his features not immediately identifiable as one of them. The bartender refused to make him a *mojito*—rum, club soda, lime juice, a sprig of mint. Domingo got a warm beer instead. In the hospital, wounded and with a couple of medals to his name, he hadn't been treated right either. The nurses had been as tight with him as one of their overtucked sheets.

The problem wasn't exclusive to the U.S. Army. Four years ago, he'd been arrested by a policeman in Guantánamo for practicing "negritude"—all because he'd let his hair grow into an Afro. *Por favor.* His mother had taken one look at the precinct captain,

whom she'd happened to have delivered, exceedingly
jaundiced, thirty-four years earlier, and he'd released
Domingo without a word. Now here he was fighting
for the Americans nine thousand miles away and mistrusted by them, too.

Another driver, an Indian, also complained about
the unfair treatment. Emory Plate said his father had
been a famous stargazer back in New Mexico, that
he'd known when sickness would claim a child or a
ewe would lose her litter, that people had come from
everywhere to see him. Emory said he wished that
he'd paid more attention when his father had talked
about starlight. Now his old man was dead a year and
who understood anything about their lives?

In Cuba, Domingo had learned that the white set-
tlers in North America had murdered most of the
Indians, that they'd killed off their buffalo, millions
of them roaming the Great Plains, that the Indians
were partitioned off on reservations, aimless and
mad-eyed. Domingo's teachers had taught him this,
teachers who'd spat when they said *yanquis,* teachers
who'd made him do the same.

He remembered the time those same teachers
had asked everyone in school to pray to God for ice
cream. Monday, Tuesday, Wednesday, Thursday they'd
prayed. Then on Friday, the teachers had encouraged
them: "Now pray to El Comandante and his great
humanitarian revolution for ice cream." A half hour

later, the assistant principal arrived carrying two huge buckets of vanilla.

One night over drinks, Domingo told Emory how he felt trapped between obligation and pleasure. How Tham Thanh Lan would threaten him one minute, then go down on him the next. How the force of his need pulled him down. Domingo was on his seventh beer. His eyes were watery, his hands unsteady. Back home, his uncles could polish off quarts of a fermented pineapple brew that unhinged even the most stalwart drinkers. They'd called it *el crocodilo* because when you least expected it, the liquor snapped you in two.

The next day Domingo went to the army library with a lingering hangover. He wasn't much of a reader, but he longed for a cheap distraction. The first book he checked out was *So You're Pregnant!* Domingo learned that human fetuses reached the size of a rosebud by three months, that fat deposits settled under their skin by six. He tried to picture his child's still-blind eyes, its ear buds and fingers with their little whorled tips. By seven months it'd be covered in vernix caseosa, a cheesy wax that would protect its skin the way grease protected ocean swimmers. Domingo had trouble imagining the baby any bigger than this.

That night, as he studied Tham Thanh Lan's enlarged body, Domingo grew frightened. How could he become a father? He hadn't been able to protect his own father, much less finish being a son. Tham Thanh Lan was in the kitchen boiling water for tea. She sat at the table, lost in thought, stirring her tea until it got cold. Now and then, she looked over at Domingo and smiled.

Coño, what did he really know about this woman?

If only everything could stop, remain fixed and knowable for an hour. Instead everything raced forward, unrelentingly, like a river, never settled or certain. Sometimes the same Vietnamese phrase stomped inside Domingo's head: *Chêt rôi.* Dead already. A hook in his mouth like one of his river fish. Maybe what he needed was a rip cord out of his whole damn life.

Domingo started checking out other books from the library—cowboy stories, a volume on tropical diseases, a history of the American Civil War—the more remote from his life, the better. He turned down poker games, stopped throwing dice, put his money away in an army savings account. At the Vietnamese waterpoints, where the other drivers went for a quick wash-and-service and two-dollar lays in the refreshment shed, Domingo kept reading.

He read *A Child's Book of Saints* nine times. Domingo admired the way Saint John had refused King Wenceslaus when he'd demanded to hear his wife's confession. Prison, torture, Saint John kept his mouth shut.

At times he wondered what the men from his first platoon were doing back home in Brooklyn and Omaha, St. Louis and Tuscaloosa. Was Lester Gentry still running numbers for his father? Had Joey Szczurak gone back to college, or was he shooting heroin instead? Were they watching the war on the evening news now like everyone else? What did it matter, anyway? They'd all die sooner or later, slowly or mercifully, emptied of light.

On the last day of August, Domingo showed up at Tham Thanh Lan's apartment with a ten-dollar box of chocolates. He didn't find her there. It was hot and humid, and the mosquitoes were pitiless. After a while, Domingo ate the chocolates, but he had difficulty swallowing them. His throat felt stripped and raw. He feared that he was forgetting something important, something that could change everything. His ears ached from listening so hard to nothing.

There was an orange on the kitchen table. He sat down and peeled it with his pocketknife. The thick rind scented his fingers. He remembered that his father had told him that in 1857, the year Chen Pan had arrived in Cuba, the price for a Chinese coolie was 150 pesos. One hundred fifty pesos for eight years of a man's life—that is, if the *chino* lasted that long. In twice that time, Domingo figured, his own son would be grown.

His legs grew numb from sitting. He stood up and jumped in place, felt a prickly sensation return to his feet. He began pacing the apartment. Suddenly everything seemed small to him, cramped like a little cage—the toy bed and coverlet, the kitchen table no bigger than a drum. Domingo felt huge in contrast, a giant, especially his hands.

What was he meant to do? He wanted to know, whatever it was.

Domingo felt in his pocket for his great-grandfather's spectacles. He polished the lenses with his shirttail and put them on. Papi had told him that Chen Pan's eyesight had been excellent until six months before he'd died. Domingo looked at himself in the mirror over the bathroom sink. The middle of his face looked perfectly clear, but he was blurry around the edges.

He closed his eyes, still wearing the glasses, and saw his father on the day they'd left Cuba. Papi had been wearing his white linen suit and Panama hat, a red carnation in his lapel. He'd held tight to Domingo's hand during the short flight over the Straits of Florida. When they'd arrived at the Miami airport, Papi's hat had been confiscated for harboring tropical fleas, and so he'd immediately bought another one, his first purchase on *yanqui* soil.

For a moment, remembering this, Domingo felt exalted, at peace, as if he could rest an eternity. He cried out with gratitude.

"Papi!" he shouted. *"¡Aquí estoy!"*

But when he opened his eyes, his father rose out of sight, high and slow, like a home-seeking ghost. Domingo imagined a flock of geese accompanying him, graceful and sonorous, their stout wings stirring the breeze. How his heart flowered with tenderness! And in the pale air behind him, Papi's Panama hat floated like a peaceful omen.

At daybreak Tham Thanh Lan appeared. Her hair was in disarray, and the hem of her *ao dai* was muddied and torn. She held up a rickety bamboo cage filled with crickets she'd collected along the Saigon River. She was nearly eight months' pregnant.

"Breakfast?" Domingo joked, half relieved.

Tham Thanh Lan didn't answer. Instead she imitated the crickets' song by pressing her tongue to the back of her front teeth. She insisted that Domingo accompany her to the Giác Lâm Pagoda. The temple was the oldest in Saigon, three miles by foot into the Tan Binh district. The weather was sweltering.

Domingo thought of the army morgue he'd visited in Danang this time last year, the stink of embalming fluids, the dead naked men stitched up like crude science projects. It had taken him two days to eat anything after that.

At the entrance to the pagoda, a statue of Quan Am, the Goddess of Mercy, stood on a lotus blossom. Tham Thanh Lan slipped off her sandals and gestured for Domingo to remove his shoes. She led him past hundreds of funeral tablets and an army of gilded figures he didn't recognize.

Candles burned everywhere, each one a little vote for change. A pot of white lilies wilted sleepily in a corner. Domingo recalled all the petitions buried by the roots of the ceiba tree in Parque Martí, a myriad of wishes and talismans. His mother always prayed under the sacred tree before going to work. *Araba iya o,* she'd greet the mother ceiba, and ask it for blessings in bringing forth life. On her way home, she'd give the ceiba thanks for another job well done.

Domingo tried to think back to what he'd wanted once, some essential need. When he was nine, he'd run along the beach near Santiago. The Revolution had been only a month old. His father had warned him of the dangerous undertow, of the rip tides that had claimed unmindful lives. But all he'd seen was the waves breaking steadily, predictable as pleats.

He'd kicked up sand as he ran, harder and faster, before diving into the sea.

Domingo shielded his eyes from the glare of the candles. The wax gave off a scorched smell. Yesterday he'd emptied his entire savings account at the base. One thousand and twelve dollars. He wanted to give it all to Tham Thanh Lan, to count it out for her in a pile on her kitchen table, to promise to send more every month. He needed to go away, to leave her like another country.

Tham Thanh Lan took his hand and led him to the figure of the Thich Ca Buddha as a child, dressed in yellow. "This is *mi hijo*," she told the young god, clutching her enormous stomach. Then she lowered herself to her knees. She wanted Domingo to swear his loyalty to her, with this god as her witness. He began to pray—not to the Buddha but to Ochún, on account of the god's yellow robes:

> *Madre mía, dueña de todos los ríos del mundo*
> *donde todo hijo de santo va bañarse para*
> *recibir la bendición del agua dulce . . .*

Tham Thanh Lan bought a finger's width of scented kerosene for one of the forty-nine lamps on the altar that was strewn with miniature Bodhisattvas. The kerosene, she told Domingo, would burn with her wish for their happiness. She wrote their names on a scrap of paper and attached it to a branch of the altar. Domingo's shirt was soaked with sweat, but his skin felt cold, like a just-caught fish. He heard the senseless rush of his own blood.

The toll of a bronze bell rolled through the smoky temple, ascending slowly, carrying Tham Thanh Lan's prayer to heaven.

It was dusk when they returned from the temple. Tham Thanh Lan went to bed still dressed in her *ao dai*. Outside, the rain came down hard and slanted by the wind. Lightning lit up a distant patch of purplish sky. Warblers quarreled loudly in a nearby banyan tree.

Domingo watched himself watching Tham Thanh Lan from a distance, like a ghost on the other side of a riverbank. Noiselessly she breathed in the darkness, slept the radiance of a doubled life, oblivious to the clumsy circling of moths, to the rain, to their ruin. Her tiny feet began paddling the air. *And so you go, never to come back.* Did he imagine her saying that?

He stood by Tham Thanh Lan's window and imagined it multiplying, stretching into the sky, a conga line of shuddering glass. Maybe there should be a kind of reality salsa, with songs for death, for silence, for forgetting. Domingo envisioned thousands of couples dancing tightly and quietly, reliving unspeakable sorrows. Wasn't failure, if spectacular enough, an achievement in its own right?

Before the sun rose, Domingo planted the cash in Tham Thanh Lan's apartment. He stuffed her mattress and kitchen pots, lined her silk slippers, folded the biggest bills in her Hong Kong jewelry box. She would find it all in ten minutes, if she looked. He wanted to leave her something more, a burning, a stamping, some proof of his faith. Then he remembered their son.

On the street, the first soup vendors were arranging their charcoal fires. The air was damp and clear. Laborers in blue uniforms raced by on their ancient bicycles. A thicket of peddlers made their way to the Cholon market carrying baskets of guavas, mangosteens, chickens, and snakes. Domingo bought a bowl of hot scallion noodles in broth. The soup tasted good, scalding and spiced with chile peppers. He paid the soup lady with his last Vietnamese coins and left.

LAST
RITES

The Spirit wants only that there be flying.

—RAINER MARIA RILKE

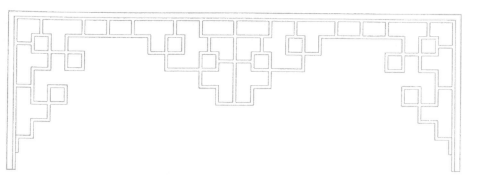

The Egg and the Ox

Chen Fang

**SHANGHAI
1970**

The guards are beating the prisoner again. The same woman who tried to commit suicide last summer by sharpening her toothbrush against the cement floor and plunging it into her wrist. The poor thing wails half the day, fraying everyone's nerves. Other times she laughs so hard the guards beat her senseless.

I've been here for three years. The cold wind freezes the bars of my cell. Dust swirls through the cracks in the walls. My every breath is a cloud. In the mornings I wake up with a pressure in my chest, as though a horse were pressing its hoof to my breastbone. Soon winter will return with its merciless jewels. The world is not what it was once. The stars are off course, loose and aimless in the sky. Here it is always dusk.

I do not think anybody expected me to last this long. Too genteel, they sneered. Too corrupted by Western ways. I am seventy-two years old. My hands are stiff, reddened with arthritis from months of wearing handcuffs. My gums are black and bleed continuously. To eat, I must first press the blood from them.

Twice I've been hospitalized—once for pneumonia, another time for rectal hemorrhaging. I fear I may have a tumor. To relieve myself is an anguish. Still, I must eat. There is only rice gruel, sometimes an extra mug of hot water when the kind female guard is on duty. Yesterday, the fat guard dislodged my shoulder when she twisted my arm high behind my back.

My interrogations come in flurries. Two or three times daily for a week, then nothing for months. My tormentors parade death before me, thinking this could frighten me. They do not realize how much more tempting it is to die than to stay alive. Perhaps there is someone on the other side already calling for me: *Come along now, Chen Fang. We are waiting for you. Everything is better here.* Perhaps eternity is just one of many possibilities.

Of course, my impassivity ignites the interrogators' fury. They scream close to my face, spraying me with spittle. "Confess! Confess!" How tiresome it is.

My eyesight is failing. The guards broke my reading glasses my first day here and they are still missing a lens. This morning an autumn leaf blew into my cell from the prison yard. Its crimson and yellow colors dazzled me. I held it close to my face and carefully turned it over, tracing its delicate veins. Its presence comforted me, as if it were hoarding a precious light.

The sound of rain washes away my most desperate moments. But anything more than a drizzle is a problem. In June my cell flooded, grew fluorescent with mold and mosquitoes. Dampness blackened the floor and a fungus grew overnight in my slippers.

Most days I try to exercise my arms and legs, clean my bed linen as best I can. I reconstruct poems in my head, patiently collecting each syllable. It pleases me to reclaim a few lines. Here is a fragment I recovered from a poem of Meng Chiao's:

A sliver of moonlight cast across the bed,
walls letting wind cut through the clothes,
the furthest dreams never take me far,
and my frail heart returns home easily.

I like to remember the mountains on summer days—the sun hanging like a stone, the black-necked crickets filling the air with their small worries. Endless days, idle and blessed. The stream surged down the mountainside with its cooling purpose, polishing rocks, and the baroque little owl waited in the eaves of the scribe's hut for its mice. Often the wind blew so hard it felt solid against my skin, like a block of wood.

Last month the kind female guard asked me to write a poem for the occasion of her son's birth. "This way I'll remember you when you're gone," she whispered. She is a homely woman with a downward droop to her nose. I know she does not mean to be cruel. The other guards kick and push me until I fall to the floor. They take away my food before I finish (I cannot hurry my meals due to my gums). But this guard gives me ample time. I am not a poet, but I wrote something for her son.

As a woman alone, a teacher of literature, I lived simply, learning to endure absence like a continual thirst. I longed for my father in Cuba, for my kind older sisters, for the touch of my beloved Dauphine. In China women do not stand alone. They obey fathers, husbands, their eldest sons. I lived outside the dictates of men, and so my life proved as unsteady as an egg on an ox.

When the Communists took over, they threw out the foreign teachers in our school: Dieter Klocker, our choral director; Serendipity Beale, the British historian who taught me to play cribbage; the biologist Lina Ginsberg, who'd come to Shanghai to escape the Nazis and married a Chinese scholar. The new leaders claimed they did not want such teachers burdening the students with alien ideas.

At first I was permitted to stay on at the school (renamed the Glorious Motherland Middle School). I did my best to implement the policies imposed upon us by Party officials and to fulfill my academic duties. Once a week an army officer would come to lecture my students. "You must plant gardens with bayonets!" he shouted again and again. What could I possibly teach them after that?

I recounted for them the story of Li Kuang, the scourge of the Huns. One night Li Kuang got drunk and mistook a stone for a tiger. Determined to kill it, he reached for his bow and quiver and shot the "tiger" with his arrow. The next morning Li Kuang found that his arrow had penetrated the stone, feathers and all.

"Given pure will," I told my students, "stone swallows feathers."

But I am not certain they understood this tale. The new generation, I fear, is largely without history or culture, boys and girls weaned only on slogans. Guns have taken the place of intellect. In the old days, it was not unusual for millers to blind the mules they used to turn their grindstones. Is this what we have become? A country of blind mules? Where are the ideas that took a lifetime to comprehend?

I miss our old language, its capacity for subtlety and consolation. And yet I am the lonely one here. These days, everything old is to be destroyed: old customs, old habits, old culture, old thinking. Teachers used to be venerated. What am I now? A dirty scrap, barely human. Too old to bother killing.

When the latest terror began, my own students beat me with sticks. They forced me to kneel for hours at a struggle meeting in the school auditorium. The president of the student body, Niu Sheng-chi, accused me of favoring the children of Chinese capitalists, of insisting upon bourgeois decorum in the classroom, of criticizing the Red Guards through clever allegory.

Others, sadly, followed suit. My fellow literature teachers reported that I introduced students to contaminating foreign authors (Kipling, Dickens, Flaubert). The mathematics instructor accused me of brainwashing young minds to think for themselves (the irony of this made me laugh aloud). Even the janitor and the groundskeeper were recruited.

Many of my neighbors were obliged to participate, to indict me for imaginary sins. I saw Pang Bao, the violinist who lived in the apartment next door, bow his head in shame during the proceedings. Dozens, however, joined in the shouting and slogans: "Dirty running dog!" "Capitalist roader!" "Spy!" What choice did they have? The kerosene seller, I noted, shouted with particular relish. I asked myself: Is contempt not the underside of envy?

I lifted my eyes and imagined a forest before me instead of this shortsighted, cowardly crowd. I remembered the storms in the mountains, how the lightning cracked and struck the tallest pines, how the wildflowers released their last sweetnesses to the wind. After the tumult, all grew quiet again. As I knelt there, humiliated, I tried to trust the larger world beyond this inconsequential gallery.

I was charged with being a Kuomintang spy, of working for French intelligence, of engaging in decadent behavior with the enemy (I wondered what they knew about Dauphine). I was denounced as a friend to foreigners, forced to wear a dunce cap scrawled with "cow's demon and snake spirit," made to repeat quotations from Mao's *Little Red Book*. Li Po wrote of such men *who have made slaughter their own version of plowing.*

"I have done nothing wrong," I repeated, hunched in my dirtied clothes. For me, those five words were my brick wall.

As the accusations against me grew wilder, my best student, Lao Mei-ping, defended me. She was a slight girl with confident hands, inclined toward the sciences. For her courage I heard she was sent to a labor camp in Manchuria. No one knows what has become of her.

I was reassigned to menial work in a factory. I filled cans with the red paint used for denunciation posters. After my home was destroyed, my books burned, my photographs confiscated (these would later be used as "proof" of my foreign connections), another family was transferred to live with me in my two-room flat.

Seize power. Every ignorant, frustrated person in China has taken this phrase to heart. *When the earth shakes, snakes slither from every crack in the dirt.*

I finally know of my son. I read about him in the Party newspaper they distribute to the prisoners. Lu Chih-mo has made his reputation running an important southern province. A reputation, no doubt, built on corpses. Of what use, I think now, was it for me to educate so many children when my own son has turned out a barbarian?

I read every article about Lu Chih-mo, trying to discern how he still might be a part of me. I study photographs of him, find the set of his mouth disturbing. When he was a baby, his lips used to quiver as he nursed himself to sleep. And when he cried, his cheeks flushed a scalded-looking red.

It is said that Lu Chih-mo is a confidant of Mao's

wife. Years ago, everyone in Shanghai knew her as a minor actress of easy virtue. I met her once at a French embassy party, provocatively dressed, on the arm of an ambitious petty official. Now she alters people's lives like theater scenery, eliminating whomever she wishes.

I know that if Mao were to lead my son to a cliff by the sea and command him to jump, he would stupidly plunge to his death. As it is, many thousands have killed themselves. They jumped off buildings or hanged themselves when the Red Guards came. Instead of one hundred flowers blooming, we have ten thousand bloody corpses, ten thousand pairs of vacant eyes.

Lu Chih-mo's personal campaign is to destroy the country's ornamental flowers, which he berates as a bourgeois preoccupation. I am told that nothing is left of Shanghai's fine gardens but dirt and mud.

I have thought of using my son's name to help me get out of prison. But what would become of him if it were known that his mother was a traitor? Would he have to shoot me to prove his allegiance to the Revolution?

Here in my cell, I live in my body more familiarly than before. Once my body existed outside me, like a musty dress in the closet. Now each new discomfort brings it recognition and sympathy.

I like to pretend that Dauphine is still dancing with me to one of her Cuban boleros. I smell the gardenia she's pinned behind my ear, her breath against my neck. I sing the lyrics as she laughs at my clumsy pronunciation:

> *Fuí la ilusión de tu vida*
> *Un día lejano ya*
> *Hoy represento el pasado*
> *No me puedo conformar*

My father must be dead by now. In the last photograph he sent us, he is wearing a cream-colored shirt and a parrot is perched on his shoulder. Father wrote that the bird's name was Jade Peach and that it could whistle twenty-six Cuban tunes. For this, too, I am in prison. Because my father was a foreigner.

I understand that everything in Cuba has changed since his time, that his country is experimenting with a similar madness. For what else can one call the subjugation of millions to the will of a troubled few?

Listen to me. I am old and very weak, but I want to live in the world again.

This is my plan. If I survive, I will search for my family in Cuba. There is a street called Zanja in the eastern part of Havana where the Chinese live. Surely someone will have heard of my father, Lorenzo Chen, the fine herbalist? And I must teach myself

Spanish! Who knows if my Cuban family can speak Chinese?

When I arrive, I will find a balcony overlooking the sea and watch the bats pour through the city at dusk (my father mentioned this in one of his letters). I will smoke a Cuban cigar (these are famous even in China), maybe two cigars. The rains will begin, splattering the city, replenishing the sea. Only then will I go inside and write to my son in Shanghai.

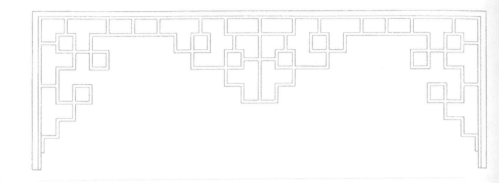

Immortality

HAVANA

(1917)

When it rained, the drops tap-tapped the broad leaves of the banana trees. Chen Pan thought it cruel to live so long, plagued with a failing body and a first-rate memory. He used to think forgetting was the enemy, but now oblivion seemed to him the highest truth. Arturo Fu Fon, who was old like Chen Pan but no longer cutting hair, liked to say, "Chen Pan, find your immortality in drink!" Then Arturo would lift his glass high in a toast: "Let us dissolve the sorrows of a hundred centuries!"

So Chen Pan drank. Red wine. A sweet Cuban *riojo.* He never touched the Spanish stuff. Not after what they did to Cuba.

It was the third Friday in August and very hot. Chen Pan sat in front of his antiques shop wearing a wide-sleeved shirt and pantaloons. His hair was fine and white and tied in a queue. The sun had burned off the morning fog, and the fronds of the palms looked rusty in the heat. A *negro,* all rags and bones, swept the sidewalk with a spindly twig broom.

Chen Pan had woken up again with cock's-crow diarrhea. Lorenzo insisted that he was suffering from a weakness of spleen *ch'i,* that there was excessive dampness inside him. This was why his gums were sore, his abdomen swollen, his legs webbed with varicose veins. Chen Pan pushed his new spectacles up his nose. Lorenzo had insisted upon these, too. A bother they were, but at least they sharpened the edges of things.

The front wall of the Lucky Find was freshly whitewashed and its sign painted red in both Spanish and Chinese. But Chen Pan didn't deceive himself. He knew he was no longer so important in Chinatown. Younger, stronger men had surpassed him, achieving what was unthinkable when he'd first arrived in Cuba sixty years ago. Now Chinese owned hotels and restaurants in several cities, laundries and chains of bakeries stretching from one end of the island to the other. Last year three *chinos* had bought a sugar mill in Matanzas and quickly doubled its output. To Chen Pan, news of the mill in Chinese hands was more gratifying than any other success.

The other merchants on Calle Zanja were too busy to visit him anymore. They rushed about fretfully from here to there, chasing riches and man-made distinctions, like Chen Pan himself did when he was younger. This knowledge came too late; how quickly the days flickered and were gone. The sun glinted off Chen Pan's pocketknife, a gift from his grandson Meng. It had three blades and a little corkscrew, scissors, a nail file, and a strange-looking device that was meant to clean out his ears.

Chen Pan was convinced that the air in Havana was growing thinner. Why else could he hear only torn wisps of sounds, as though the air were muffling every disturbance? At times, he barely heard his own voice reciting his father's poems. *Tether the sun on a long rope so that youth might never pass.* Chen Pan thought it odd that he could still remember this line but forget his father's face, or what his hands looked like holding a book.

And who would remember *him* in fifty years? What was the point of enduring life, raising it up like a great bell only to see it crash to earth? Everything that mattered today, Chen Pan decided, that seemed serious and important, would vanish tomorrow. Was there no end to this meaninglessness?

At the barbershop, the younger merchants liked to imagine the world a hundred years after they were dead. They spoke of men flying to the moon in over-sized balloons, of reproducing themselves without women (although everyone objected to this!), of in-gesting vitamins instead of rice to survive. Chen Pan listened to them with bemusement. How could they imagine death at their age? It was obvious they thought of themselves as *ch'ien-li-ma,* thousand-mile horses, who could run forever without resting.

Life's details might change, Chen Pan told them, but the essence of it would remain the same: long stretches of misery broken by intermittent happiness and the fear of death.

"Bitter old man," the young men scorned him. "You belong back in China."

Arturo Fu Fon, who'd remained a bachelor all his life and to no one's knowledge had ever sired a child, said the key to a good life was desiring no more than you could use. This alone, he maintained, ensured contentment. Chen Pan hadn't heard a better pre-scription from anyone.

Nine years ago, Arturo Fu Fon had returned to China. He'd spent a great deal of money and traveled for months, but when he arrived in his village, he found that there had been an epidemic of dysentery and his entire family had died. Arturo Fu Fon emptied his pockets and bought candles and incense for the deceased. Then he took the next ship back to Cuba.

Over the years, other friends of Chen Pan's had returned to China. They'd taken the ferry to New Orleans, then a train through miles of dusty plains to the western coast of America, and from there a ship for the voyage across the Pacific. It was an expensive trip, but Chen Pan could have afforded it. Lorenzo had promised to accompany him if he ever decided to go. But where would he go? Whom would he visit? Why would he travel so far just to scratch a bit of long-depleted earth?

Except for Arturo Fu Fon, those who'd returned to their villages had boasted of having three or four wives, twenty children or more. *The more cows, the richer the man!* Chen Pan knew these men viewed him as foolish, still in love with a dead woman. "You can't warm yourself against ashes," they'd admonished him. Everyone had expected Chen Pan to have more wives, many children. It showed strength that a man could satisfy a young wife, keep producing sons. It was a disgrace to grow old alone.

To this day, his friends teasingly compared him to the revered widows of China, who worked miracles through the force of their virtue. (They retold the story of the widow from G——, who cut off both ears to save her honor and was rewarded by heaven. Her ears grew back during the next rainstorm!) Was Chen Pan, they chided, counting on performing miracles in Havana with his record celibacy?

But Chen Pan thought them the foolish ones. Did they think their young wives hadn't noticed their thinning hair and dried-up faces? Would death be dissuaded by so much confusion and noise? Chen Pan suspected that every last one of them was fed up with his wives, his homes, and his children and would have preferred nothing more than to be left alone. So why would they want him to share their fate?

From his pocket, Chen Pan pulled out what was left of the sky-blue dressing gown that had belonged to his wife. The gown was in tatters, the neckline torn, but he wrapped the fragment around his wrist. For ten years the nightgown had held Lucrecia's original scent—a peppermint and sea-salt odor—before it had gotten musty with old tears. It was true that his love for Lucrecia had grown with each passing year. Chen Pan was astonished at its persistence. Who was it who said: *If only one person in the world knows me, then I will have no regrets.* So why was he so regretful?

Chen Pan imagined taking a small blue boat and

sailing it beyond the rim of the horizon, beyond the slowly rising sun to where he knew Lucrecia's spirit rested. Last March, he'd bought a revolver and polished it every day. He couldn't decide whether to go on living or simply shoot himself. Sometimes he spun the revolver on the nightstand or on the counter of his shop, waiting for it to stop and point at him directly. It never did.

What did it mean to die, anyway? What if there wasn't a shred of truth to anything he'd learned? After all, who had ever returned from the beyond to inform the living?

Chen Pan marveled at the optimism of others in the face of death. Their insistence on pasting paper money everywhere. Or burying their loved ones in three coffins, one inside the other. Or inserting bits of mercury-dipped jade into the orifices of the deceased to delay their decay. What if death was no more or less than this: the *ka-pling* of a broken string? Each time Chen Pan thought about this, he felt as if each hair on his head was on fire.

Recently, the young merchants of Calle Zanja had convinced him to sit for a portrait. They'd wanted paintings of all the old-timers for their new associations building. Chen Pan had found it wearisome to sit still. Why had they wanted to immortalize him now, wrinkled as he was, his face like chewed sugarcane? Why trace his withered limbs on silk? "You should save your rosy paints for the young beauties of Chinatown!" he'd rebuked them.

Every day Chen Pan heard of this one or that one dying, another losing the power of speech. All his closest friends—save Arturo Fu Fon—had passed to the land of the ghosts. A few had suffered overly long: tumors grown to coconuts in their stomachs; legs cut off from too much sugar in their blood. There was a sad, scraping sound to all their partings. Last month, Fausto Wong had died at the age of ninety-three after eating fifty-six dumplings in one sitting.

Chen Pan regained his humor only when his youngest grandson visited him. Little Pipo was already five years old and looked just like his father. The boy wore two-toned brown shoes buttoned on the side, and his shirts were a gosling yellow. While it was true that Chen Pan was getting harder of hearing every day, his grandson's face, so liltingly animated, more than compensated the loss.

Chen Pan liked to entertain Pipo with stories of Lu Yang, the warrior who had divided night from day by shaking his spear at the sun. Or of the incorrigible Monkey King, who'd stolen peaches from the Immortals' sacred grove and eaten his fill. "The most important thing about life is to live each day well," Chen Pan told his grandson, who looked up at him, perplexed. "In the end, you'll have a pattern. And that pattern will speak more than anything you can remember."

Most days, Chen Pan settled with Pipo on the outdoor rocking chair for an afternoon nap. How sweet it was to feel his grandson's plump cheek pressed against his chest.

By late morning, the street vendors were aggressively vying for sales. Chen Pan watched one limping *guajiro* hawking a live pig slung across his back. A bedraggled farmer drove his goats from door to door, milking them for customers on the spot. How much longer, Chen Pan wondered, would their worlds last?

Just before noon, Lorenzo came for a visit, wearing his yellow doctor's smock. The family parrot was perched on his shoulder. Everyone knew Lorenzo in Havana and in other cities as well. It was because of him that in hopeless cases, the Cubans said, *"No le salva ni el médico chino."* Not even the Chinese doctor can save him. Three years ago, Chen Pan had broken his ankle chasing a pickpocket. His son had coated his foot with *bai yao* and expertly wrapped it in flannel. Before long, Chen Pan could have kicked his heels together in the street.

In May, Chen Pan had accompanied Lorenzo and

Pipo on a trip to Sagua la Grande. Lorenzo had grown renowned for a potion that restored a woman's virginity, and his services were urgently in demand. Lorenzo had developed the formula from a weed he collected in the Zapata Swamp. His patients placed a teaspoon of the lavender powder, disguised in bottles labeled VITAMINA-X, beneath their tongues for a week preceding their nuptials. Miraculously, it produced a bloodstained sheet. Lorenzo reported that lapsed society girls and their relatives paid him generously to save their families from disgrace.

Chen Pan had taken Pipo to Calle Tacón in Sagua la Grande's Chinatown, which bustled with shops selling incense, puppets, firecrackers, and the honey-peanut candies he loved. He bought a bag of the sweets to share with Pipo and together they watched the Cantonese magicians in the street. He overheard one criollo commenting on the Orientals' hypnotizing skills. *It's part of their religion, more dangerous than the Haitians' voodoo. If you look them straight in the eyes, you're doomed.*

Chen Pan knew that many of his son's clients also went to him for weakness of sex. Lorenzo complained that all these men wanted was to remain stiff, like soldiers saluting, for hours. What choice did he have but to procure the essential ingredients? Carcasses of wild donkeys. The dried penises of seals and sea lions (which he ground into potency powders). Tips from the tails of red-spotted monkeys. Lorenzo supplemented these with an elixir derived from the *yagruma* tree, which stimulated his patients' circulation.

"Let's see your middle," Lorenzo said, leaning forward.

Chen Pan lifted his shirt and submitted to a cursory examination by his son. He wondered whether he could still please a woman the way he used to please Lucrecia, pleased her so well she'd loved him day and night.

"History is like the human body," Lorenzo said, tapping Chen Pan's stomach, "overly hot or cold or rotting with stagnation." He spoke of a longevity root called *heshouwu* that could keep a man alive 130 years or more.

"Now don't go sneaking any of *that* into my tea!" Chen Pan bristled. He was eighty years old. His biggest fear was that he would live so long he would turn to stone. How could he trust his son not to use some decoction to lengthen his life?

"Don't worry, Papi." Lorenzo laughed. "You're the last person who needs it! I was thinking of taking it myself!"

At one o'clock, Chen Pan's daughter-in-law arrived at the Lucky Find with sweet-corn soup and a firepot of steamed fish and vegetables for lunch. Chen Pan called her *bing xin,* pure heart, and was grateful for her visits. Around her everything smelled and tasted of China. Next month Jinying would bake mooncakes for the mid-autumn festival and offer their ancestors choice morsels of meat to win their favor through the coming winter. Chen Pan remembered how Lucrecia had learned to bake these same mooncakes for him. She'd tried everything to please his Chinese side until slowly she'd become Chinese herself.

Chen Pan returned to the front of his shop to read the Chinese newspaper. Over the years he'd followed the reports of the Boxer Rebellion and the lengthy decline of the Manchus. First Sun Yat-sen had been president, then Yüan Shih-k'ai had replaced him. Now warlords ruled China again. Chaos and violence reigned, just like when he was a boy.

After so many years in Cuba, Chen Pan had forgotten much of his Chinese. He mixed his talk with words from here and words from there until he spoke no true language at all. There were only a few people left in Havana with whom he could comfortably communicate. Long ago he'd lived in China, known all its customs and manners. How useless these had been outside their own geography! Still, it was easier for him to be Cuban than to try to become Chinese again.

Today, he concentrated on the foreign news. There was a revolution in Russia and a war between Germany and most of the world. China had sent troops to the Western Front to dig trenches, bury cadavers, do the work no one else would do. In Cuba the war meant the price of sugar was soaring. In times of misery, there were always profits to be made. Chen Pan knew this better than most. With every disaster, his secondhand shop flourished.

Not long ago, President Menocal had passed a law allowing more Chinese immigrants into the country for the duration of the war and for two years beyond it. Boatloads of *chinos* were coming to the island to work the sugarcane fields again. Lorenzo sent Meng to the port every morning to pass out notices advertising his herbal services.

Chen Pan knew it was only a matter of time before the Chinese no longer would be welcomed in Cuba. In times of economic necessity, they were usually the first scapegoats. This infuriated Chen Pan because thousands of *chinos* had fought hard for the country's independence. During the Ten Years' War they'd taken up machetes, fought under Calixto García, Napoleón Arango, all the great leaders.

They'd stayed long years in the war, too, not like those criollos who swelled the ranks after news of a victory and disappeared when the losses began to mount. *Chinos* fought everywhere in the eastern provinces—in Las Villas, Quemado de Güines, Sierra Morena, San Juan de los Remedios, Camajuaní. When they were captured, they pretended to speak no Spanish, but not a single one ever surrendered or betrayed the Cuban cause.

When Chen Pan had delivered his fifty machetes to Commander Sian back in 1868, the battlefield had been littered with torn limbs and severed heads and the Spaniards' fallen, heaving horses. Chen Pan helped round up supplies from the corpses—swords, muskets, boots, and numerous trumpets. Overhead, vultures drifted patiently, waiting for their turn at the carnage.

Before long, people from town had come to dance with the rebels and blow the stolen Spanish horns. They roasted a pig under the taper-lit trees and drank a local *aguardiente* that fire-burned their throats. A former slave entertained them with impersonations of the rebels. He told a joke about a Chinese *ayudante* who served the troops fresh-roasted chicken after every skirmish.

"How do you find so many chickens in the woods?" one soldier asked him.

"¿Tú quiele pollo?" the Chinese cook retorted. *"Mata capitán pañol."* ("You want chicken? Kill a Spanish captain.")

That night Chen Pan had gotten drunker than he'd ever been in his life. When he passed out, the skies were so dense with stars that he tried to reach up and grab a handful.

Chen Pan watched the setting sun bronze a royal palm. Laundry fluttered among the crumbling buildings. A glossy Pekingese sniffed its way down the street wearing the oversized collar of a circus clown. A dragonfly drifted by, trailing its gauzy world. To see a thing for the first time, Chen Pan thought, was better than to know it.

It was at this hour that he saw his errors most clearly, the days he'd wasted in empty pursuits. If only Lucrecia had lived longer. Without a woman, *yang* ruled a man's blood. Life became a horse without reins. Strength had to be balanced with weakness. How else could stability be bred?

To spend his regrets, Chen Pan went to the cock-fights with Arturo Fu Fon. They preferred the pit near the Regla ferry. Everyone—blacks, *chinos,* and criollos—gathered there for the best fights in the city. *"¡Mata! ¡Mata!"* they shouted until the arena shook with violence. After the fights, the handlers spit rum on the heads of the victors and blew alum into their eyes to stanch the bleeding.

Chen Pan wished he could go to the pit every day, but it wasn't easy to arrange. Recently, Arturo Fu Fon had begun falling asleep unexpectedly, sometimes in midsentence. One minute he might be talking or grinning his toothless grin and the next, loudly snoring.

And for no reason Chen Pan could discern, Arturo Fu
Fon frequently covered his face with his hands like a
woman, as if to shame somebody.

C hen Pan climbed the stairs to his rooms
over the Lucky Find and poured him-
self a cup of wine. He watched the night settling over
Havana and wondered whether anything new was
possible. The city, it seemed to him, conspired to sad-
den him with its daily repetitions. The nine o'clock
cannon shot. The church bells ringing every quarter
hour. The watchmen mechanically shouting the time
and the state of the weather.

As the bats swept along the rooftops, Chen Pan
remembered the cranes that had nested in the eaves
of his great-aunt's house, the spring chives she'd cut
in the night rain, the river lotuses that had stripped
their petals to make room for new blooms. How could
he explain this sudden longing he had for home? For
the way his heart clamored like a bird in its last
moonlight?

By now, Chen Pan knew the precise length of each
darkness. Sometimes he washed his face through the
small hours of the night until his skin appeared
translucent. Other times, he didn't wash at all. Tonight the moon seemed to shrink away to nothing,

like a fasting monk. In China it was said that a rabbit lived on the moon under a cinnamon tree, pounding an immortality salve.

The air was much too warm and close in his room. Chen Pan opened the window and saw an owl streak past, stealing the day's last moments. The old wisteria shivered on its vine. If only he could fly alongside the owl, glide over the rooftops, sleep with a cloud for his pillow.

Chen Pan poured himself some more *riojo*. He recalled his fugitive days in the forest, the long months of his mother's taunting, calling him to her eternal emptiness. Now who could walk the way he'd walked in Cuba anymore? Who could hide for three hundred days, avoiding men and ghosts, living on nothing but memories and his five senses?

On the island all the trees had been chopped down, the land leveled and torn to plant more sugarcane. Forget the pines, Chen Pan lamented, forget the mahogany, the cedars, the indigo trees (from which he'd whittled the best and sharpest knives). Forget the trogon birds hiccuping in the canopy. Forget them. Forget everything. That island he knew no longer existed. If he could start over, would he board the ship for Cuba again?

Chen Pan poured himself another cup of wine. A few more, and he would start to feel drowsy. Perhaps he would dream of those cranes again, snow white and wheeling through the sky. Or of the white paper on his front door indicating that he'd already died. Or of the funeral curtains blowing in the storm. Or the steady wailing of his neighbors. In his dream he was shouting, his eyes fixed as a dead fish: *I want to live a little longer, my friends!*

He saw his remaining days like so many autumn leaves. The past, the present: where to end his life? Everything had vanished in the breeze. Yes, a man lived less than a hundred years, but he harbored cares for a thousand. Chen Pan took a long swallow of the *riojo.* It seemed to him that he'd been waiting all his life for this very cup. Soon, he thought, the roosters would rip open another day with their battling cries. But his friend hadn't lied. When Chen Pan drank his red wine, he smiled and became immortal.

ACKNOWLEDGMENTS

Ongoing thanks to my friends and generous readers: Scott Brown, Wendy Calloway, Mona Simpson, José Garriga, and George de Lama. Special thanks to Philip Caputo, Hanh Hoang, Evelyn Hu-DeHart, and Kenyon Chan for their excellent suggestions, to Norma Quintana for her sisterhood, and to Leonard Comess for his kind wisdom. And finally, *mil besitos* to my daughter, Pilar, for her humor and sweet forbearance, and to my goddaughters, Caridad and Grace.

Cristina García was born in Havana and grew up in New York City. She is the author of *Dreaming in Cuban,* which was nominated for a National Book Award, and *The Agüero Sisters.* Both novels have been widely translated. Ms. García has been a Guggenheim Fellow, a Hodder Fellow at Princeton University, and the recipient of a Whiting Writers' Award. She lives in Santa Monica with her daughter, Pilar.

A NOTE ON THE TYPE

The text of this book was set in Century Schoolbook, one of several variations of Century Roman to appear within a decade of its creation. The original Century Roman face was cut by Linn Boyd Benton (1844–1932) in 1895, in response to a request by Theodore Low De Vinne for an attractive, easy-to-read typeface to fit the narrow columns of his *Century* magazine.

Century Schoolbook was specifically designed for school textbooks in the primary grades, but its great legibility quickly earned it popularity in a range of applications. Century remains the only American face cut before 1910 that is still widely in use today.

Composed by Creative Graphics,
Allentown, Pennsylvania
Printed and bound by R. R. Donnelley & Sons,
Harrisonburg, Virginia
Designed by Iris Weinstein